While running from the law across the New South Wales border, Will Jones and his crew join forces to stop a runaway wagon, saving the life of the terrified driver. On board, inside a tea chest, is a precious cargo – a new breed of pups that will one day become known as Queensland blue heelers. The smallest of the pups appears to be injured beyond repair. Can he be saved? The owner doesn't think so.

Pursued by a dogged but flawed police sergeant, Will continues the journey north, following river tracks with Lainey, Fat Sam and Gamilaroi Jim. On the goldfields of North Queensland they receive an offer too good to refuse. This leads them to a new field, where nothing is quite as it seems. Will Jones needs all his wits to escape the trap set for him, though it's the loyalty of his mates that saves the day.

Will Jones and the Blue Dog is the second book in the series, following on from Will Jones and the Dead Man's Letter, set across the colourful and wild landscape of 1880s Australia.

Also by Greg Barron

HarperCollins Publishers Australia
Rotten Gods
Savage Tide
Lethal Sky
Voodoo Dawn (short fiction)

Stories of Oz Publishing
The Hammer of Ramenskoye (short fiction)
Camp Leichhardt
Galloping Jones and Other True Stories from
Australia's History
Whistler's Bones
Red Jack and the Ragged Thirteen
Outlaw: The Story of Joe Flick
The Time of Thunder
The Last Days of Dom Sebastian
Beyond the Big Bend
Will Jones and the Dead Man's Letter

First edition published 2023
by **Stories of Oz** Publishing
PO Box K57
Haymarket NSW 1240

ABN: 0920230558
facebook.com/storiesofoz
ozbookstore.com

ISBN: 978-0-6453511-8-7
Cover Design & original artwork by Angus Crowley
Proof Reading: Brad Connors
Typeset in 11-point Book Antiqua
Printed and bound in Australia by IngramSpark

Will Jones & the BLUE DOG

by Greg Barron

Chapter One

The Runaway Wagon

1886 Southwestern Queensland

That old echidna was no fast mover, but he ambled along the stony earth with his stumpy legs moving in a hunched over left-right rhythm, a layer of red dust powdered over the brown of his quills. He'd scented a termite mound over yonder, near where the mulga started. These termites, he could tell, were plentiful and active, and he was keen to lick them up with his long, sticky tongue.

It was late afternoon, and the burning orb of the sun was easing down towards the earth, though the ground still hoarded its warmth. The echidna had spent the day in his burrow, sleeping and dreaming of juicy termite nymphs and succulent queens. Now, finally, he was on the hunt, hungry and single-minded.

Abruptly he stopped; his snout twitching, the sensitive receptors there telling him that he had come to a road. The wagon ruts were deep in places, formed back in February when the northern wet season had dipped south from the tropics and dumped five inches of rain in a couple of days. The echidna remembered it well, for his burrow had partially filled with water.

He sniffed again, and set off across the road.

The echidna was halfway there when he sensed a vibration in the ground, barely noticeable at first. He felt it in his nasal passages, in the hollow spaces of his quills, and even his claws. He had seen and heard human vehicles in the past, always at a safe distance, and was able to identify the sounds of spinning wheels and of hooves on earth.

If he'd hurried, the old echidna might have made it across the track, but that opportunity passed. Instead, he looked up and with his tiny eyes saw two horses drawing a wagonette, heading directly towards him. On the driver's box was a wild-eyed man, and he was yelling at the horses.

Frightened now, the echidna rolled himself into a ball and gripped the earth with his claws so tightly that no jaws, hand or talon would ever lift him. He heard more yelling, and the thunder of hooves. Even in his protective ball, he was frightened. Fortunately though, it didn't take long before the sound moved on and away down the track.

Feeling safer, the echidna opened his eyes and lifted his head, only to drop it again, terrified. Three horses, all with riders crouched in their saddles were galloping towards him at a breakneck pace. These were, he was sure, the fastest-moving animals he had ever encountered in his life.

Down went his head until they too had passed. After a minute or two a third rider came, leading a string of horses at a more sedate pace.

Still the echidna waited, until finally the vibrations faded into the distance. Now the old fellow eased his claws loose, lifted his head, then committed to the crossing. His mind again turned to the feast of termites that would soon make up his evening meal.

***

Almost a mile ahead by then, Will Jones was coming up to the out-of-control wagonette at a gallop, urging his gelding to approach the offside horse, while Lainey did the same on the opposite side. Will's hat flew from his head in the slipstream and he hoped that Fat Sam would pick it up for him as he brought up the horses.

Will could see the reddened, terrified face of the driver, but even worse the wheel of the wagonette was wobbling like a shearer on a spree and it was obvious that it would soon part ways from the vehicle. Up ahead the track degenerated into a gibber plain of rocks, most of them as big as two clenched fists. It didn't take a genius to predict that the crazed horses might lose their footing on the stones and the rickety wheel shatter or slide from the axle.

Coming up to the offside horse Will saw that foam had begun to fly from its nostrils, and that sweat coated its hide.

'Try for the bridle,' Will shouted to Lainey, who he could see on the other side.

Lainey didn't answer, but he saw that she was already leaning inwards from the saddle, reaching with her left hand and holding the reins with her right, calling soothing words to the horses. 'Come on, darlin's, slow up now.'

Will was doing the same, but with more force and no less finesse, taking a grip on the bearing rein, his own horse starting when its thigh touched the shaft. But now, with a rider on either side, each with a grip on the harness, Will and Lainey exerted slowing force with the weight of their own mounts. This effort, together with Lainey's pleaded words of comfort, was causing a gradual slackening of pace.

With enough time now to look, Will saw that Gamilaroi Jim was parallel to the wagonette, attempting to climb from his horse onto the vehicle. As always he wore long grey dungarees and no shirt at all, the muscles standing proud on his dark skin. Jim took a grip on the wagonette hoops, climbed from his horse, and slipped down next to the driver.

'Good work,' called Will.

Now they hit the first of the rocky ground, and the offside wheel parted ways from the wagonette. The whole vehicle sunk to one side and skidded. Jim held himself and the driver in place by dint of his strength, while Will and Lainey concentrated on slowing the horses and preventing another panic. All in all, the thing was done with a good measure of control, and finally the wagonette, and the horses that drove it, stopped in a broiling sea of dust.

For a moment or two, no one moved. Men, woman and animals alike remained still, chests heaving. It was as if they were collectively worried that a single word might panic the runaway horses all over again.

Finally, Jim and the driver of the wagonette half-fell, half-climbed out of the steeply sloping vehicle, reaching the ground and dusting themselves off.

Will looked at the driver curiously. He was full-bearded in the same shade of white as his hair, with a compact body and long limbs that made him seem spider-like.

'Dear Gawd in 'is 'eavenly throne,' the driver said. 'I swear that I can't thank you people enough. If you 'adn't a' come along in time I cannot guess what might'a 'appened.'

Will backed his horse a length or two, to give the man some room. 'We were in the right place at the right time, and that's for sure. I'm Will by the way. That's me sister Lainey, an' Jim were the one what jumped on board the wagon with ya.' Fat Sam was just coming up with the packs and spare horses, also carrying Will's lost hat and leading Jim's horse. His eyes took in the scene with his usual calm. 'This quiet barsted 'ere is Sam – you can see that he's Cantonese, but he's one of us.'

'Darn pleased to meet you all. Me own name is Scotty McCrae – part owner of Mudie Station thirty mile yonder. All this 'elp is unexpected but most welcome.'

'Got to help each other out in the bush,' said Will. 'But tell us, will you, what startled the poor bloody horses off in the first place?'

Scotty made a face, then spat heavily into the dust between his feet. 'Oh it were a darn fool anteater – echidna or whatever ya call 'em. I tried to swerve around, but that didn't help. The horses didn't like the look of him an' went straight into a bolt.'

Will accepted the explanation. 'Well, it's a good thing we were follerin' so closely behind. It's too late to move on now, so we might as well set up camp back before the rocks start. We just passed a creek bed that should have a hole or two – we can help you get these horses to water and in the morning we'll put that wheel back on.'

'That's nice of you, sir,' said Scotty. 'I've plenty of tucker, 'an' I can use a saucepan better than most.' He bowed low, 'I'd be 'onoured to prepare a slap-up feed for all of youse tonight.'

In the silence that followed this promise there came a strange sound from the back of the damaged wagon. Will imagined that it might be the squeal of a rat at first, but then it came again – once, twice, then a third time. It was a yap, a bark, yet from an animal too small to deliver any depth to the sound.

'What the hell is that?' asked Will, but Lainey, who always beat him hollow in the curiosity stakes, was already dismounting from her horse and walking towards the rear of the wagonette.

Chapter Two

Inside the Tea Chest

Scotty McRae hurried to the rear of the wagon, and with Lainey looking over his shoulders he lifted a wooden tea chest down to the dusty track, opening a lid into which many holes had been bored, and looking deeply into the interior. 'Oh Jesus, the poor little beggars,' he said.

Lainey held a hand to her chest and made a soft sound in her throat that sounded like concern mingled with amazement.

Curious about this development, Will dismounted and handed his reins to Sam. Then, walking up to the chest, he too stared inside. He saw three furry bundles – pups of course, but of a breed he had not seen before. Their coats were blue, flecked with darker shades, and white too – beautifully patterned.

Unfortunately, the shock of the wagon lurching to its axle had not been kind to the pups. One of the three had blood around its nose, and had left a blotch of red against one wall of the chest. Another was crying pitifully, trying to walk unsuccessfully. The third seemed to be unharmed.

Scotty picked the one with the bloodied snout up by the scruff of its neck and lifted it close to his face. 'You alright there big fella?' Then to Will and his sister, 'Just a nasty little knock, I'd say.'

'I could get a cloth with some spirit on it to clean his nose up,' suggested Lainey.

'That'd be a big help,' agreed Scotty, and he passed the pup across to her, careless of a new daub of blood on his sleeve.

The next pup began to yelp as soon as Scotty picked it up. Changing his grip he cradled the animal's belly in his palm, and felt along its ribcage with the other forefinger. 'Oh bugger – feels like he has some broken ribs. Darn it, he was such a nice little fellow too – I call this one Little Blue.'

Will felt a twinge of unhappiness at this, 'Oh that's a bloody shame, the poor little mite.' He peered up close at the injured pup. 'I've never seen a dog like these ones before.'

'They're a new breed,' said the driver. 'A mate of mine's been experimentin' with the 'usbandry. They're calling them the blue cattle dog – originally a cross between a blue merle collie, dingo and some dalmatian. Some people call them Hall's Heelers after the bloke who first bred them, or Queensland Blue Heelers but the official name is gonna be the Australian Cattle Dog.'

'They really are blue,' Will marvelled.

Scotty smoothed back the pup's ears, which seemed to help calm the animal's cries for a moment. 'Yeah, and the breed is second to none – loyal, tough, smart, and better with cattle than most English breeds. I was taking these three back to me own farm. Sad it's only gonna be two now.'

Will was shocked at this announcement. He inclined his head at the pup in Scotty's hand. He had more striking markings than the other two: a white blaze on his forehead, black masks around both eyes and a daub of tan for eyebrows. 'You're not gonna put him down, are you? Won't them ribs heal up?'

'I doubt it, but I s'pose I can try – we don't want 'im to suffer though. I'm no animal doctor but if we bind him up it might 'elp.'

'I'll get a clean shirt and make some strips,' said Will helpfully, and it was one of his own shirts he sacrificed to the cause, using his sheath knife to cut and tear three long strips from the tail.

When he returned they wrapped the little dog's middle up tight, then encouraged him to drink a little water from a saucepan lid on the ground. Will stood, watching the damaged little creature try to stand and lap the cool liquid, wondering why his heart ached so hard.

***

Within an hour the horses were watered and hobbled, grazing on the sparse grasses, bells clunking gently as they moved. Night had fallen by then, but the moon was already high, and Sam had a good fire that provided its own flickering glow.

The wagonette itself was not yet repaired, but they had lifted the left side, slipped the wheel back onto the axle then repacked the load. In the morning Jim, who was a dab hand at such things, would finish the repair.

Fat Sam had a good fire roaring, and Scotty McRae was making good his promise to cook. He had beef that was still fresh enough to eat once the pale outer skin had been trimmed away. Two of the three pups eagerly ate the trimmings, and made nuisances of themselves around the camp. The biggest was called Noah, always first to the food, and seemingly unconcerned by the small cut on his snout. The sister was Molly, almost as big, but not as enterprising.

Little Blue, with his broken ribs, had been confined to the tea chest, in the hope that he might not strain himself, and fits of his wheezy yelps mingled with the call of a nearby stone curlew.

When the meal was over Lainey had Molly in her lap, and even Sam was enjoying Noah's antics around the camp. Will said to Scotty, 'Can I get the poor little barsted out?'

Scotty looked at him strangely, then, 'Why yes, a'course you can.'

Will opened the lid of the tea chest, picked up Little Blue, and carried him back to his spot beside the blaze. He was wearing the blue serge jacket he had once won in a card game with a naval officer. The little dog seemed to forget his injuries for long enough to be attracted to the brass buttons, worrying them with his teeth until Will gently moved him away.

'Now, now,' he said. 'I don't want to be sewing any of them buttons back on again.'

'Count yourself as lucky,' said Scotty. 'These blue dogs don't warm to strangers easy – even at that age. He's taken a shine to you.'

Will held the dog on his lap while Scotty recited a poem he had penned, a song of the brown scrub and the red earth of places west – the lowing of cattle strung out along the track, dingos howling near lonely campfires. Gamilaroi Jim followed up with a yarn that seemed not the least bit fantastical on that sullen red terrain, of spirits in the watercourses, and silent things that move across the outback skies on cold winter nights.

Fat Sam smoked his pipe with his usual dedication, and Scotty seemed interested in his Cantonese background, and why he had hooked up with such a carefree crew as this.

'Will you go back to China one day, do you think?' Scotty asked.

Fat Sam shook his head. 'Never go back,' he said.

Scotty cracked a grin, 'What'd you do, kill someone?'

Sam looked away, ignoring the question, and there was no hint of a smile on his face.

***

Later, when the fire had burned low but was not yet out, Will woke in his swag, hearing the sound of whimpering from the tea box. It cut through his heart like a bowie knife.

He lay rigid in his swag for ten or more minutes, then muttered to himself something about 'keepin' the little fella warm.' He got up, walked to the tea chest and lifted the pup with the little belt of bandages, and carried him to his swag.

At first the animal still whimpered and tried to burrow into his warmth. Will felt a cold nose on his cheek, then the sandpaper lick of a tongue. The little dog crept in under the blanket.

'You're a funny bugger, aren't you, Little Blue,' Will said under his breath. 'Shame you had to go and get hurt.'

Worried that he might roll and hurt the dog, Will was determined to remain awake, listening to every harsh breath and whimper. There was no doubt that the pup was struggling with pain on each breath.

Through the long early hours, when the moon had sunk to leave a black sky spread with stars, he willed the little dog to survive.

***

The next morning, with the wheel repaired, and two calm and rested horses in the traces, Scotty packed the last of his things in the wagon and prepared to leave. The three pups went into their wooden chest, and Will held Little Blue for as long as he could, before placing him in with his brother and sister.

The little pup would not take a feed that morning and Scotty had sighed. 'Little Blue might be injured inside 'is gut, the poor little beggar. Things don't look too bright for 'im.'

Will was surprised at himself for feeling melancholy at seeing the pup go. 'I hope he heals up alright,' he said.

'So do I.'

'They'll love being at your place, I'm sure,' Will went on. 'Learning to muster and such. Maybe we'll drop in one day and see how they're getting' on.'

'I'd like that,' said Scotty. 'In fact, can I offer you some work? We can always do with a few more men in the stock camps?'

Will thought for a moment. They were still less than a hundred miles from the border with New South

Wales, where there was a price on his head, and a couple of days ride from the scene of a man's death that they had watched with their own eyes, and did not particularly want to be questioned about.

'Not just now,' he said. 'We're hell bent on seeing some of the country up north, but maybe next season.' Will couldn't help but let his eyes drop to where the pup he had shared his swag with was looking up at him with eyes that seemed less bright than they had been the previous afternoon.

'I don't have a fortune in cash on me,' Scotty said, 'but will you take a couple a' bob for the assistance you gave me yesterday?'

Will shook his head. 'No chance, old mate, you cooked a top feed and the company of you an' the blue dogs was worth every minute. Now get on the road and take those pups home. Hopefully all three will soon be chasin' around like they're meant to.'

They all shook hands, and swore to meet again. The wagon set off at a sedate pace, rattling on the stones. Will suddenly felt like it was going to be a long day, worried sick about what would happen to the little dog he had felt such a connection to.

Chapter Three

Hard Decisions

'P'raps you should have taken up that job offer,' said Gamilaroi Jim as he, Sam, Will and Lainey rode north along the Adavale road. 'We could do with a quid or two, an' Scotty seems like he'd be a good boss.'

'Nah,' said Will. 'The plan is to head north so let's stick to it.'

Normally he might have said more, but instead he rode in silence, while Gamilaroi Jim ambled his mare along nearby, bare chested as usual, repeating every bird call. When a golden whistler whistled, so did Jim. When a raven issued his abrasive caw Jim answered it perfectly. He even captured the butcher bird's pure song and the chatter of willy wagtails.

Yet nothing seemed to lift Will's spirits, and he wasn't prone to feeling low. Not even having half the New South Wales constabulary after him, for a crime he didn't commit, had affected him as much as the mortal illness of one little pup.

'What's wrong with you?' asked Lainey, her blonde hair in a ponytail extending from a hole in the back of her cabbage-tree hat. 'Never seen you look like such a misery guts.'

'Nothing wrong with me,' said Will. 'Looking forward to town – a good pub feed and pot or two of dark and I'll be right as rain.'

'I suppose we could stop an' boil the billy soon?' asked Lainey.

'Barely got enough tea left for a whiff each,' said Will. 'But I suppose we may as well use it up.'

'Hey Will,' called Jim wheeling back from his position a hundred yards ahead of them. 'Aren't that Scotty's wagon up ahead at that intersection?'

Will slowed his horse and stared, 'I think you're right. It is.'

He tried not to hurry at all, but even from a hundred yards distance he could see that Scotty had pulled his wagon off the track a way, horses still in the traces, and that he was working at a hole in the ground with his shovel, in a clearing beside a patch of bluebush.

As he came up, Will dismounted, and walked his horse in. Scotty's face was red from exertion, and it was easy to see that he was upset.

'What's up?' asked Will.

Scotty stopped digging and leaned on his shovel. 'That poor little pup is getting' worse. I'll have to put him out of his misery,' he said, 'and I figgered I'd dig the hole first – if this here ground weren't hard as concrete I'd have finished by now and been on me way.'

Will turned to see Lainey over near the wagon, where the little dog was laying on a scrap of soiled blanket, trying to sit up to investigate the newcomers. Leading his horse over, Will tethered it to the same mulga tree as Lainey had done, then walked across and kneeled down beside the stricken animal.

Scotty joined them with his shovel still in his hands. 'I don't want to have to do this, but the damn pup hasn't stopped whimpering since I left you this morn, and as you can see he's been passing stools with blood in them. The responsible thing is to end the poor fellow's pain.'

Will stared dumbly. 'You mean, put him down?'

Scotty sighed and wiped his sweat-streaked forehead with the back of his free hand, 'Yes, I 'ave to put the poor little fella to the sword, so to speak.'

Lainey looked stricken, and she turned away. 'Oh that ain't good,' she said.

'How will you do it?' asked Will, barely glancing up as Jim and Sam also tethered their horses and came in on foot.

'That's just what I were figgerin' out. That's why I thought I'd dig a nice hole for 'im first, then decide.'

Will felt for his pipe in his top pocket, packed it full of Dixson fine cut from his pouch and caught the packet of vestas that Jim threw to him. 'Don't do it, mate. Let God decide the little bloke's fate.'

Scotty face burned a brighter shade of red, contrasting strongly with the white of his beard. 'Now I don't want to get shirty with you, after the good turn you done me yesterday, but that ain't your decision to make. It's mine. I'm responsible for 'im and I don't believe in allowin' an animal a lingering death when he can have a quick one.'

Will bent to the blanket, and lifted Little Blue in his hands, cradling him against his chest. There was no doubt that the pup was less active than he had been that morning, but yet, he snuffled at Will's shirt, and tried to lick at his neck. 'He wants to live, see?'

Scotty slammed the blade of his shovel down on the ground, glancing off a stone so it made a ringing sound. 'Damn it. No!' He pointed with his free hand at the track that came off the main road, winding out to the west. 'That's my turn-off home, but I've got another night's camp before I get there. We run a rough homestead and I'll be straight out with cattle – I got no way of nursing a sorely wounded dog. Best you can do mister, is ride on and leave me to what 'as to be done.'

'He's right Will,' said Lainey. 'Let's go.'

But Will was getting in a mood of his own, leaning down to tap out his pipe and crossing his arms in front of his chest. 'It ain't right, to kill the poor little beggar like that. It weren't his fault that the horses bolted.'

Scotty's face grew redder still, and his lips clamped together. 'Don't think I dunno who you are. Everyone's talkin' about the gang from New South Wales riding north – a white, a celestial and a Gamilaroi man with no shirt. There's a troop of pinks waitin' for you at Adavale from what I've heard, led by a New South Welshman called Sergeant Douglas – who has an extradition warrant for yez all.'

'Long Douglas,' breathed Jim. 'He's follered us all this way?'

'Sounds like it,' said Will, then, to Scotty. 'So you knew all this and didn't tell us last night?'

'I only figured out who you are as I moved on this morning – you were such decent types that it threw me off the scent – I wouldn't pick yez for a murderous gang.' He sighed heavily. 'Now, for the love of Jove, take 'eed of me warning about what's waiting for you in Adavale. Get on your horses and ride away, an' leave me with this 'orrible responsibility.'

'I'll do that, but don't kill Little Blue,' said Will. 'Take him home with you.'

Scotty turned and threw the shovel as far as he could, and it landed near the hole. 'You want to save him, dash it all, then you take the pup, and see if you can perform some miracle on the poor bastard yourself.'

Will stared back at him. 'I-I can't take him. Not on horseback. Not on the run like this.'

'Well there's your choice,' said Scotty. 'Either you take him, or ride on and I'll do what needs to be done.' With those words, the station owner stalked back to his shovel, picked it up and resumed his digging. Sam, Jim, Lainey and Will stood in a circle around the dog.

Lainey's eyes flashed. 'Now you just think about this, brother of mine. You'd be takin' on a dog that's sick and in pain, with no wagon to carry 'im. Even if he survives you 'ave to be around to feed the damn thing every day, an' not let it get ate by hawks or snakes 'til it's growed enough to look after itself. Then you have to think about what Scotty said about Long Douglas on our tail. We can't ride fast and hard with a sick bloody dog with us … ' She looked down at Little Blue. 'But I do wish that he could live.'

Jim blew a stream of smoke towards the sky, then turned to Will, 'You can't even look after yerself, bloke,' he said, 'let alone a pup – specially one as crook as this.'

'I look after me horses well enough,' said Will. 'no animal 'as ever suffered in my care.' He turned to Sam, 'What are your thoughts?'

'Makes no difference,' said Sam. 'You not ever listen anyhow.'

Will lifted the pup and looked into its eyes, while the little paws scrabbled at thin air. 'What about you, little fella, are you in so much pain that you'd want it all to end? Or do ya want to take your chances with a down and out rover like me?'

There was no sound but for Scotty's shovel biting into the hard earth, and a distant raven, and they all waited for Will to speak again.

Chapter Four

Long Douglas

Further north, in the front bar of Adavale's Imperial Hotel, New South Wales police sergeant Roger Gerald Humphrey Douglas took a last, fortifying mouthful of rum from a crystal glass. Through the dusty panes of the window he could see the troop of Queensland Mounted Police who had been seconded to his command lined up outside with their horses. They were hard, bearded men, lean from living rough: Troopers Johnson, Chandler, Smith and Davies. Corporals Elfick and Dunn. The other three were trackers – Ginger, Willy and Bob. A small crowd of locals had gathered to watch the patrol move out.

'Long' Douglas, as he was known, stood up, collected his pith helmet and started to head for the door. His nickname was an ironic one, bestowed on him because of his small stature. As if to make up for this handicap he wore his tunic with upright pride, his shoes shining black and silver spurs that jangled with each step.

As Long Douglas started to make his way to the door, however, the publican appeared from around the side of the bar, blocking his path, and in his hand he held a yellow square of paper. He was an outrageously tall man, lanky as a colt, and with neatly trimmed sideburns. 'Excuse us a minute Sergeant, but I'd be obliged if you could settle your bill before you ride out.'

Long Douglas opened his mouth in surprise, 'Any expenses incurred will be settled by the New South Wales Police. Kindly direct your invoice to them.'

The publican raised the paper, 'Will they be pleased to pay for Coq au Vin, some of the ingredients for which we had to send a rider to Charleville?'

'Well,' spluttered Douglas. 'A man must eat.'

'And Bollinger champagne?'

'They will not begrudge their champion, far from home and in regions remote, a suitable refreshment after the rigours of the track.'

'Nevertheless,' said the publican. 'I require your cheque for the amount of nineteen pounds, three shillings and sixpence before you step through that door.'

Long Douglas raised himself on his toes. 'You dare to threaten an officer of the law?'

The publican did not raise his voice but there was an iron glint in his eye, 'I am not threatening you, but I aim to be paid. If you do not, I can assure you that I will send the word out, making sure that you will not be welcome in any pub in any town in Southern Queensland.'

Douglas sighed, put down his helmet, accepted the invoice and read it grimly. He reached into an inside pocket, retrieving a folded chequebook. Using the quill and inkpot offered by the other man he leaned on a bar table, still sticky with the residue of yesterday's beer. 'This is most inopportune,' he said as he scratched an amount and his signature, 'and I can assure you that my former high opinion of your establishment is now very low indeed.'

The publican said nothing, just watched as Long Douglas tore off the cheque and passed it across with deadpan eyes.

With the cheque in the publican's hand Long Douglas secured his pith helmet on his head and stalked his way out through the front doors, across the creaking, pit-sawn ironbark verandah and outside into the already burning morning sun. His 'boy' had brought his horse around and placed a stump to assist his sergeant in mounting. Once Long Douglas's rather plump behind had settled into the saddle leather, he looked out at the local people who had gathered to watch the patrol ride out – four or five of whom were noticeably drunk. A couple of others were business types in hats and waistcoats.

Long Douglas decided that the crowd would expect him to say a few words, just as a Greek hero might have addressed his fellow Athenians before riding into battle. He sat up straight in the saddle. 'Dear people of Adavale,' he said. 'I have in my possession a warrant for the arrest and extradition to the colony of New South Wales of one William Jones, his sister Elaine Phillips, Wu Yan-tou – also known as Fat Sam, and a Gamilaroi Aboriginal man most often known as Jim. The warrant is for the crimes of murder and conspiracy to murder, evading arrest and affray. In addition William Jones faces charges in the colony of Queensland for escaping lawful custody in the town of Eulo.'

There was laughter amongst the spectators at this, for the story of Will Jones's escape from the Eulo lock-up, under cover of a diversionary fire had kept the bush telegraph humming a few months earlier. One of the drinkers, reminded of this, threw an arm around one of his fellows, and hooted with mirth.

Long Douglas glared at the pair then spoke on regardless. 'This pursuit will not be an easy one. We know for a fact that the fugitives are armed to the teeth. Apart from the Snider carbines and revolvers of various makes they were already carrying, Will Jones and his companions did steal a repeating Henry rifle from the

New South Wales police.' He paused, waiting for a reaction of shock and surprise from the bystanders. There was none, unless the lighting of a pipe or two could be counted as such.

'We have outsmarted these vicious outlaws,' he went on, 'by gathering our forces ahead of their intended march, and will now cast our net southwards, to swoop them up like minnows in our net. Fear not; the force of law cannot be contained. It cannot be thwarted. It cannot be run-away from successfully.' Then, with a dramatic flourish, Long Douglas turned to his gathered troop, ten men in all, with twice that number of spare horses and loaded packs. He raised an arm. 'Come, my merry band. Let us ride forth and bring the forces of lawlessness to justice.'

By now the drunks were contorted with laughter, all but rolling around on the ground, but Long Douglas focussed instead on the town's Church of England minister, a very thin young man and his wife, who were clapping heartily. Two members of the world's oldest profession, standing oddly beside this pair, also seemed impressed.

As the patrol rode out of town, past the Divisional Board Hall, a row of houses and the first of several itinerant camps, Long Douglas reflected on how proud his mother would be of him, if she could see him leading such a formidable force as this, out into the wilderness.

A forlorn place indeed, he decided, as the track wound in and around the channels of Blackwater Creek that lay dry and dusty like an endless claypan.

His father had been a merchant – part owner of a small fleet of coastal traders. With a house at Double Bay his early life lacked for nothing. When the company flagship, the brigantine Progress was lost off Byron Bay, however, Roger Douglas's father was on board. Raised by his mother, Roger's childhood was one of books and Sydney Harbour skiffs and fishing for flathead in the little bays near their slowly decaying home.

At first apprenticed to a draper, he joined the New South Wales police force at the age of nineteen. Newly qualified, he was posted to Grafton, in Northern New South Wales, then Bellingen, Taree and Armidale. At just twenty-eight he was promoted to sergeant-in-charge at Coonabarabran. The town suited him, straddling the Western Plains, and with the Warrumbungles a dramatic backdrop.

It was there that Long Douglas first came up against Will Jones. A man who was everything Roger Douglas hated: a larrikin who people instinctively liked; a terrible thief from whom no horse was safe, and a man born to the bush, an advantage that no amount of experience later in life could seem to match.

As for the murder of which Will Jones was accused, only Long Douglas knew the truth. He took the reins in one hand and fingered the stock of his Winchester rifle in its scabbard with the other. Jones's presence at that creek bed on that fateful day was a useful accident. It was vital that he did not get taken alive; that he must not live to tell his story.

Chapter Five

The Bulloo River

When Will Jones called out to Scotty McCrae and told him that he would take the blue heeler pup and try to nurse him back to health, he had no real idea how difficult that would be.

Lainey stood with her hands on her hips. 'You're soft in the head,' she spat. 'Would Ned Kelly have taken a sick dog with 'im to Glenrowan?'

'I ain't Ned Kelly,' Will replied. 'An' I don't plan on stagin' me own Glenrowan.'

After Scotty had moved off with his wagon, however, Lainey went from angry to practical, fashioning a sling for her brother to carry the pup under his arm. Gamilaroi Jim and Fat Sam watched with bemused expressions on their faces, not wanting to say the obvious – that the animal was not likely to survive the rigors of life on the road.

Before long, however, they were walking the horses up the track, with Jim in the lead, scouting ahead. Little Blue was asleep in the warmth of his sling. Every now and then Will slipped a hand inside to feel for the animal's heartbeat, reassuring himself with its regular rhythm.

With no real plan but to skirt Adavale when they got closer, they were all a little wary of what was coming, and when Jim came riding back towards them in a hurry, Will could see by his face that he was alarmed.

'What's going on?' asked Will.

'P'lice troop – havin' dinner camp up ahead. Must be small water, for the tailers bringin' horses in one by one ter drink.'

'Is Long Douglas there?'

'Yeah, seen the little barsted there too.' Jim moved his arms and head in a parody of a rooster walking.

'He's a little cock of a man,' Will said, 'that's for sure. But e's persistent. We'd best get off the track quick smart. They'll be coming this way soon, so we'd best get to it. Jim, can you sweep our sign?'

Jim gave Will a look as if he were deficient. They all knew that no one could do it better.

***

First they rode back the way they had come until sparse kangaroo grass gave way to iron-red stones, and there they made their departure, with Jim following on foot.

Well-versed in the art of anti-tracking he used a branch torn from a brigalow tree to sweep the surface where their tracks diverged from the well-trodden centre, straightened spinifex stalks or turned stones that had been scored by a horse shoe. For a quarter mile Jim kept this up, while Sam, Lainey and Will walked their mounts, until finally the stones became sparse.

Now they performed a trick Jim had taught them. They picked out a recognisable distant landmark, in this case a flat-topped hill some three miles away, then separated, making complicated and erratic trails before meeting up again on the summit of that rise.

'That should throw them off,' said Jim as he slid from the saddle and took up a vantage point behind a great slab of stone. And while Sam held the horses Will, Lainey and Jim watched the far-off road as the police broke camp and rode by.

Will clapped his hands as the troop – fifteen men in all – continued past the point where he and his friends had detoured. 'We fooled them,' he said,

'Maybe for now,' said Jim, 'but one a' them trackers; he saw something; he went off the road a little, but the p'liceman called him back.'

Standing, brushing off their clothes, they returned to the horses, and Will poured some water into a pannikin for Little Blue, who did take a small drink, but had to be supported around his bandaged body while he did so.

'We've got decisions to make,' Will said, standing with the small dog in his arms. 'We can't go south again, and I'm not sure we should go anywhere near Adavale neither.' He turned to Sam. 'What do you think?'

Sam pointed to the west. 'Bulloo River not far away.'

'Good thinking,' agreed Will. 'We could maybe hide out there for a spell – let the dog come good again. Queensland is a fair lump of a place, an' they can't follow us forever.'

'I for one would be grateful for a river camp tonight,' Lainey said. 'It's been days since a proper bogey. Maybe latch onter a fish or two – Sam always has a line handy.'

'Yeah, that'd be a fine thing, a river camp,' said Will.

And they rode the afternoon hard through lancewood scrub and brigalow, or bare plains of bluebush and spinifex, with the yellow splash of everlasting daisies or fields of waving mitchell grass. The scene rarely stayed the same for long, and with the eyes of bushmen the differences were more apparent than they might be to a newcomer.

They reached the Bulloo before sunset and the river was a welcome and shaded sight, yet there was no feeling of sanctuary or relief. The banks had been scoured by the passage of stock, grass sparse on the flats alongside.

'Drovers been through,' commented Sam.

'Not just one,' agreed Will. 'Thousands of head, muddying the damn river, and eatin' out every last blade. I should have guessed that we'd be fair smack on a droving trail, headin' north, all that country up there every squatter has his sights on, an' this might not be the best place to hide.'

'It'll do for tonight though, won't it?' asked Lainey hopefully.

'Yeah, it'll do for tonight – any drovers nearby will be in camp by now, so they won't trouble us before morning.'

Scouting around, they found a bend in the river with a steep bank that the cattle and sheep had avoided, but a small rock ledge below that could be reached with a careful descent. Will clambered down to fetch a canvas pail of fresh water, and Little Blue eyed the river warily and snuggled back against the warmth of Will's navy jacket, with the reflections of the coolabahs and red gums all around them, and a crimson sun glaring as it hurried for the horizon.

While Sam took the horses out to find some feed, the others soon had clothes out of swags and were washing everything from underwear to shirts, scrubbing the cloth against itself, whacking them against tree branches, then hanging them on makeshift clothes lines.

Jim pulled a handful of very long and thin green leaves out of a shirt pocket and showed them to Will. 'Here bloke, try some of this on the dog.'

'What is it?'

'Gumbi gumbi – powerful medicine – haven't seen it much aroun' here but passed by a couple a' healthy shrubs up the track. Might help ya dog, bloke, but he need meat to go with it.'

'That's if he'll eat,' said Will.

'He has to eat,' said Jim, 'or we'll be buryin' him soon enough.'

***

The Snider being far too much gun for the task, Will borrowed Jim's new Henry carbine — the one that he had inherited from the New South Wales police force in the Pillaga. Leaving Little Blue in Lainey's care he wandered away from their camp, down along the bank until he came upon a wallaby that had come to drink.

Working the lever, enjoying the smoothness of the action, he took the shot offhand, aiming for the head for an instant kill and to avoid meat spoilage. The beautiful creature fell dead, never knowing what had hit it, and Will picked it up by the legs, away from the mud, and skinned and gutted it on the high bank.

Jim looked up as Will arrived back at camp, 'How many bullets it take you to kill that skinny little feller?'

'One,' said Will.

Jim made a mocking smile. 'I never seen you hit the thing you aimed at first shot in yer life, bloke.'

'Well, this time I did.'

Settling down with his roll of knives and a chopping board of Macleay ironbark, grooved by many blades, he went to work. A section of the backstraps he diced into tiny pieces for the dog, and these he mixed with chopped gumbi gumbi leaves. The rest of the backstraps he pierced with the point of a knife many times, then rubbed with handfuls of salt, tucking the result in a canvas bag. Without this preparation the meat would be close to spoiled by morning.

While the wallaby haunches roasted in the coals, Will begged, cajoled and encouraged the little dog to eat, but he would do little more than whimper and sniff. Jim watched for a bit, then asked with his eyes if he could take the dog. Will passed him across, and watched Jim's big, dark hands gently handle the animal. Leaning over, he took a lump of Will's meat mixture between his fingers, then rolled it into a ball. He used his free hand to prise open the little dog's jaws, and thrust the meat deep inside with his finger. The pup struggled for a moment, then recovered.

'You try,' said Jim. 'Just a little bit more.'

Will, a little disturbed not to have thought of such a neat trick, took back the pup and mimicked Jim's actions, and by now Sam and Lainey were both watching too. He took a lump of meat and herbage the same size as Jim had done, and opened the dog's mouth. He didn't get it down quite as far as his mate had managed.

'Close 'is mouth and stroke it down,' said Jim.

This worked also, and when Will offered the water dish the pup lapped up more liquid than he had all day. It was encouraging, and it was a happier camp as they risked building the fire up for light and warmth and chewed fresh haunch meat and were grateful for it.

Yet Will was not feeling safe enough to abandon all caution, and they agreed to draw straws to keep watch. Lainey, drawing the easiest, early shift, walked out after sunset with just a revolver in her belt, heading for a small rise nearby.

Later, however, just as Will was thinking of unrolling his swag, there was a shout from Lainey out in the darkness: a challenge. Then the voice of a stranger echoing amongst the coolabahs.

Chapter Six

The Drover

The stranger strode out of the darkness of the riverside canopy, with Lainey close behind. He wore stained moleskin trousers, 'elastic-sided boots and a striped shirt. His hair was dark but a little thin, plastered to his head from a day of sweating under a hat, though he was now bare-headed. He was leading a long-legged stock horse by the reins, a poley saddle on its back. Following warily was a short-haired collie, distrustful of this strange camp, choosing to sit at the edge of the firelight and pant softly.

'Welcome, stranger,' said Will, coming to his feet, turning to signal to Sam with a tiny shake of his head to put away the carbine he had trained on the man as he entered the camp. 'Come and warm yourself. We have a little wallaby meat, if you're hungry.'

'Why thank you,' said the stranger, fixing his eyes on Will, 'but I've just ate a good feed of mutton an' johnny-cakes. We've a mob two mile ahead, and we're missin' half a dozen ewes – came scoutin' down for them and seen yer fire. Figured I'd find out who it was.'

'Which way are you headin'?' Will asked.

'North. Up to a run west of Blackall – two thousand maiden ewes and a hundred and fifty rams. We're Liverpool Plains folk originally, but these lot are from another run we own out near Burke. Ted White's me name, by the way.'

'Well damn it all,' said Will. 'Liverpool Plains? I know a White family from the range country south of Willow Tree. Arthur White is an old mate of mine.'

The drover cracked a grin. 'Well, Arthur's me own brother – would've been along on this drove if his missus wasn't expectin' a third. Now I'm guessin' that you're the famous Will Jones – I ain't seen you since you were a young tacker.'

'That's me,' Will said, 'here, tie up your horse an' stop for a yarn.' Sam left the carbine lying on his blanket, and as if to apologise for his hostility, he took the reins himself, and secured the horse nearby.

Ted White thanked the quiet Cantonese for this courtesy, then squatted down near the fire, fumbling in his top pocket for a pipe and the makings. 'None of us could believe our ears when we heard you was wanted for murder.' He turned to Lainey, 'You must be Elaine, is it?'

'That's me.'

'F'give me if I stare a bit, but I ain't seen a good lookin' sort like you for many a long week.'

'Oh, I don't mind so much,' said Lainey. It was a while since Will had seen his sister's face turn red, but it now took on a shade of crimson that a fresh slice of beetroot would have envied.

'Do you know the country up ahead?' Will asked.

'Well enough, I've done this trip half a dozen times, over the years.'

'Then I'll pick yer brains, if you don't mind,' said Will. 'We're aiming to amble up north, but we need to hide out for a few days.' He waved a hand to where Little Blue was asleep on an old jacket near the fire. 'We've got a sick pup, an' need somewhere we won't be disturbed. Is there any place you know where we can lay low for a spell?'

Ted White, having packed his pipe, lit up from a burning stick and drew deeply. Dogs, in his world, were a valuable commodity – a good one was worth two men – and the idea of changing plans to nurse one back to health made perfect sense to him. He considered the idea for a moment or two then snapped his fingers. 'Oh yeah, Hellhole Gorge, on Powell Creek. It's part of Milo Station, and the stock route skirts it, but there are a couple of waterholes up in the stone country where it aren't easy to take stock and you won't get bothered.

Best of all most of the Queensland trackers won't go near the place – it has a sad history – a bad history. You'd be safe enough there for a few days.' He paused to smoke in silence for a few minutes, then his eyes lit up. 'Here's an idea. If you can be in the saddle at first light, an' catch us up, we'll tuck you up in front of the mob. No tracker that ever drew breath could find a spoor after a thousand odd sheep have walked behind you.'

Will looked around at the others. 'That's the best blasted plan I've heard all day,' he said. 'Now help yourself to what food we have. If only we had a bottle of rum to share with a mate on this night.'

'No rum needed,' said the stranger, 'an' I'd best ride on and find them sheep. You'll see us along the left bank – as early as you can get there.'

***

In the morning they rose with the sun still just an underglow in the east, and Little Blue seemed a little better, eating several more lumps of meat mixed with herbs, even taking most of these on his own, along with a healthy drink of water.

An hour later Will, Jim, Sam and Lainey were making their way around the mob, greeting the drovers with their dogs on the wings, moving across the sunshine of the morning feeling as safe and protected as they had ever been. The pissy smell of sheep was almost overpowering, but as familiar as home, and the bleating a comfort rather than an annoyance.

The mob moved slowly, less than a mile an hour, and when they went into dinner camp Jim became restless. He rode ahead, reaching as far as where the cook had driven his wagon to set up for the evening.

That night they shared the drovers' camp, well-stocked as it was with flour and tea. They sat around a hearty fire, sharing yarns, talking of the bush, and far distant places. Ted made no secret of his admiration for Lainey, but he was nothing but gentlemanly and considerate towards her.

Little Blue had begun to take an interest in his surroundings and there was a moment of hilarity when Midge, Ted's Collie, sniffed the injured pup out, and the two dogs, young and old touched noses. The bitch must have known that the little blue dog was poorly, for she licked his side solicitously, then left him alone.

'Might be able to take them bandages off tomorrow, bloke,' said Jim. 'Help him move around if he wants to.' No one dared to say it, but the little dog seemed to be out of real danger and on the mend.

Later, when Will went to his swag, a small fire burning beside him for light and warmth, he took a postcard from a leather case that hid his cash and most precious documents. He spent a full minute staring at the girl whose photograph appeared in the postcard. He did not know who she was, just that he loved her and no other woman would do. She had become his silent obsession. He put the postcard carefully away before laying his head on the pillow and closing his eyes.

Will, like the others slept without fear of traps or discovery, nor even the horses straying, for there were men on watch throughout the night. In the morning the four of them assisted with catching horses and the cook provided a good breakfast before they headed out, once again enjoying a day of riding at the head of the mob.

Late on the third afternoon, after hours of dry saltbush country, the drive reached Powell Creek – not so much a waterway as a parched sheet of rock. There was a hole downstream a little, for the sheep had scented it and were hurrying in that direction. While the other men watered the mob Ted White rode in to talk to Will and the rest of the group, Midge matching pace with his horse.

'We have to part ways here,' said Ted, keeping the flies from his face with a swipe of his hands, but if you follow the creek bed upstream, you'll reach the gorge country. Find a quiet spot and I doubt anyone will bother you.'

There were handshakes all round, and Will swore that one day he'd pay back the many kindnesses Ted and his mates had shown. 'Just one thing before we leave,' Will said. 'You say that the trackers won't go near this Hellhole Gorge. That something bad happened there. What was it?'

Ted shook his head. 'I dunno much about it. Just that a station owner called Welford was tomahawked and speared fifteen or so year ago, not too far west of here.' He then jabbed a thumb upstream. 'They say that Hellhole Gorge is where the Native Police and a posse of landowners caught up with the Kungkari people that done the murder.'

Jim showed his horror on his face, and Will shook his head slowly, as if to clear an unpleasant thought. 'I don't blame the trackers for not wanting to go there then. But it still sounds like a handy place for us to hide out for a bit.'

Leaving the droving party was a wrench – it had been nice to be amongst a crew that had adopted them as friends. Now, however, it was time to regroup, and bring the little dog back to full health. With Will in the lead, they turned away up the creek, and slowly the sounds of bleating sheep and the smell of the mob receded into the distance.

When Lainey turned around and saw Ted still watching after them, she blew him a kiss.

'What'd you do that for?' asked Will. 'He's got it bad enough for you already.'

'The poor barsted deserved it,' said Lainey. 'An' if he'd had a bath in the last six months I would'a done more than blow a kiss.'

'Yer a married woman,' growled Will.

'Not to my mind I ain't,' she said. 'Most boring years of me life, they were, bein' the little woman. I'd rather be an outlaw, any day.'

Will scowled and urged his gelding into a trot, heading out to the front, horseshoes clumping on the hard stone of Powell Creek.

Chapter Seven

The Trackers

Long Douglas and his patrol had ridden on for the rest of the day after missing Will Jones and his crew south of Adavale, heading down through Bulloo River station country: Bull's Gully, Glencoe and an outstation of Milo called Tintinchilla.

By late afternoon, after many uneventful miles, Long Douglas had his sights set on the homestead at North Comongin, just an hour's ride ahead. He had shared a table with one of the station's owners, a man by the name of McLean, in Eulo a few weeks earlier, and he had seemed like a very nice fellow indeed – had offered shearer's quarters for the men and a room in the house for Douglas himself if the patrol happened to come through that way.

The comforts of a homestead, which apparently also boasted a very scenic billabong, appealed to Long Douglas far more than a night in camp. He pictured in his head a meal of hot lamb roast, gravy and potatoes, the station missus solicitously pouring his drinks and admiring his uniform.

Up ahead, in defiance of his haste, he spotted the patrol's three trackers off their horses and in earnest conversation. This, surely, was an unnecessary delay to a hot bath and meal. Outraged, Long Douglas urged his mount into a trot.

'What in heaven's name is going on here?' he demanded as he came up to them.

The three troopers turned to look at their sergeant, then continued to talk amongst themselves in their own language. This casual disregard, along with the fact that he couldn't understand a word of what they were saying, infuriated Long Douglas, and he was a man capable of instant transformation from calm to rage. He made a scoffing sound in his throat. 'Excuse me. Did you happen to hear the ranking officer give you an order? Now, mount your horses and take the trail.'

Again they ignored him, despite the fury in his eyes and the spittle that flew from his lips. Douglas dismounted from his horse, and hurrying forward, grabbed the nearest of the three trackers by the hair. This was no mean feat, for the man was at least a head taller than he was. The man squealed, reeling backwards in the direction of the hair-pull.

'Now that I finally have your attention,' spat Long Douglas. 'I told you to take the trail.' He gave the man's hair a last tug then pushed him in the back. Preparing to mount his horse again, he was surprised to see the man making no move to do the same. 'Thunder and damnation trooper. If you want a thrashing, you're going the right way about it. Never in my life have I seen and heard such insolence. You've got three seconds to mount up and take the trail.'

'Trouble is sergeant,' said the tracker, 'that the trail don't go this way no more.'

'Then where on earth does it go?'

The tracker pointed to the north. 'Sometime back Mister Will Jones leave the road.'

'Damn your eyes, are you telling me that we've been following a cold trail?'

The tracker inclined his head, cringing with his eyes and lips as if knowing that his revelations would bring on a tantrum from Long Douglas.

'What's your name, Trooper?'

'Joseph, sir, Trooper Joseph.'

'How much of a bonus were you promised for this venture? A shilling a day was it?'

Again he nodded.

'Well kiss today's shilling goodbye, for you and your incompetent brethren. We'll ride on to North Comongin and start retracing our steps in the morning.'

The white Queensland police constable called Benny, lounging on his horse throughout the exchange, said,

'Beggin' your pardon, sergeant, but I can't see the use in ridin' another ten miles onwards, then having to come back this way again first thing tomorrow. Trooper Joseph here was sayin' a minute ago that he thinks he might know where we missed them, and it were a fair ways back – we could make up some lost ground now – there'll be enough starlight to get by, and the moon will rise soon enough. Then we could go into camp not far from the spot and have an early start at them.'

Long Douglas turned on the tracker furiously. 'Why didn't you tell me that you saw something.'

'I try to Sergeant, and you call me back.'

Long Douglas stuck his foot in the stirrup and swung up onto his horse, shifting uncomfortably in the saddle. Being made to look in dereliction of his duty was even worse than having to camp rough – and they had passed a public house of sorts up the track so the night may yet be passed in comfort. 'Very well then, we'll ride back the way we have come, but this oversight will be mentioned in my report, Trooper Joseph, and you can expect a reprimand from your commanding officer when the time comes.'

***

Twenty miles to the north, a little after ten the following morning, Long Douglas watched Trooper Joseph work in concert with his two mates. It took them an hour of searching to find the place where Will Jones and his gang's spoor had stopped. This done, they began to cast around for the spot where the fugitives had left the road, narrowing it down to the edges of a gibber plain.

The sergeant was in a better mood than he had been the previous afternoon, having taken a room at a roadside pub operated by a Scotsman called Gunne. It was little more than a shanty, really, but the food had been hot, the mattress soft, and the liquor hard. Long Douglas prided himself on his head for drink. He had risen at dawn, with scarcely a hangover, and joined his patrol, who were camping outside, in time to rouse the stragglers out of their swags.

Trooper Joseph turned to look at the sergeant, smiling. 'This feller a clever one,' he said, then tapped his own head with a forefinger. 'Proper good puzzle.' And he kept his head low as he led the way across that plain of stones. One clue at a time: a scuffed rock; a bent grass stalk. Clues that were only visible to Long Douglas when Trooper Joseph or one of the others pointed it out.

When the stony expanse ended the single trail became four, and several hours of unravelling multiple threads followed. It was noon when Trooper Joseph showed Long Douglas the rocks on the hillock from which the fugitives had watched the police patrol ride along the road.

When they reached the river, the spoor was complicated by drovers and their herds coming through. Even now the last of a northbound mob of cattle were strung along the Bulloo pools, hereford and angus breeders moving slowly, urged along by tough men on tougher horses.

Once the mob had moved on the three trackers separated, and while Long Douglas waited in camp with the billy boiling and damper on the coals, they scouted up and down gullies, in dense thickets and along the banks. Finally, the sharp eyes of Trooper Joseph won through. He found a two-day-old camp on the western bank, and rode back to fetch the sergeant and corporal.

The tracker pointed out the earth-covered fireplace, along with the prints of boots and bare feet in the dust. 'Three feller camp here.' And a small distance away he pointed out a smeared black stool on the ground. 'Little dog,' he said. 'Sick-fella.'

Long Douglas smiled to himself. Now it was only a matter of speed. With twelve armed men they could not fail to overcome Will Jones and his little band when the time came.

Chapter Eight

The Hellhole

Over a full day of riding upstream along Powell Creek, the weather changed from a sun-fired burning heat to a different kind of discomfort. A greasy layer of cloud stole across the sky from the north, and with it came a clinging, broiling humidity that kept up day and night. Shirts were drenched, and sweat ran in trails down Jim's bare dark torso. When Lainey tucked her dress into her pantaloons no one had the energy to comment.

They found more than one waterhole along the creek, and several times Will, Jim, Sam and Lainey yarned from the saddle, discussing the merits of the place as a campsite. Will, however, was looking for true solitude, and he urged the others to ride on. This area, Ted had told them, was part of the vast Milo Station, and there were signs of stock and the cold fires of their keepers here and there.

Finally, however, they had to dismount to deal with increasingly wild terrain. Leading their horses they

58

reached a small but deep waterhole, surrounded by craggy shelves of orange and grey stone. With no more signs of people or stock this looked like the perfect place to regroup, and for the little dog to heal.

In many ways this was a beautiful camp. It was certainly dramatic, with turkey bush amongst the stone faces, bright red lolly bush fruit and even fuchsia flowers where soaks bled from the cracks and dampened the soil. A pair of Major Mitchell cockatoos in a river red gum watched them come, a little wary at these unaccustomed visitors, and a brace of turtles dived into the deep.

Yet, for all that, it was a brooding place. An uncomfortable place. And there were other, more deadly creatures here.

As the travellers dismounted, they disturbed a big old mulga snake, and she lifted her blunt head, riven by the tessellated plates of her scales. Her tongue came and went from between hard lips, tasting their scent in the air. She viewed the interlopers with calculating eyes. It wasn't often that humans came to these stony reaches. Reluctantly she left her favourite place on the warm stone and slithered away into the crags before they saw her. For all the two decades of her life she had been queen of this place. Two-legged visitors were not welcome.

***

'I don't like it here, bloke,' Jim said to Will as they lifted saddles from their horses and unburdened the packs. 'Especially after what Ted said had happened here. I can almost see the ghosts.'

Will did not disagree. 'I know what you mean, but those old dead warriors got no complaint with us. They won't mind us hidin' out from the traps on their country.'

Jim made a face, 'That Long Douglas is on our trail, I can feel it. Two nights here, maybe three, and no more. We have to move on.'

'I agree,' said Will. He knew Jim too well to dismiss his instincts.

***

Fat Sam was an artist with the fishing gear, and few things made him as happy as tying one of his needle-sharp hooks onto his catgut line, wound around an old rum bottle. After catching a pocketful of grasshoppers for bait, he threaded one wriggling specimen onto the hook and crouched at the edge of the pool, a study in concentration, one hand extended over the water, the line held by his forefinger.

That night they ate small grunter fish cooked on the coals, and for the dog Will prepared balls of fish mixed with dry gumbi gumbi leaves. Now, it seemed, the pup needed little encouragement to eat. He wolfed down the flesh as fast as Will could prise a lump off the backbone and roll it around to check for bones.

Then, long after the four had retired to their swags, Little Blue was restless, and Will tried to keep him still. Yet, there were things in the night the pup did not care for.

For just outside the firelight, that big old mulga snake slithered along the edges of the camp. Every inch of her was hard-country muscle, forged on rock and dust. Her fangs were hollow needles; her venom potent enough to kill a bullock.

***

The second day Little Blue was looking much better. He was beginning to scurry around the camp, and he had an appetite to match. Wandering off to look for meat, Will found a lost Milo ram in poor condition and alone. Having separated from the flock the animal had somehow evaded the many dingos in the area. It seemed to Will like a mercy when he dropped the animal with the Henry rifle.

Later, Will saw Jim working away at some greenhide.

'Not like you to be doing any work,' Will commented, lighting his pipe and squatting down to watch the other man's nimble fingers.

The Gamilaroi man sneered, 'I can work the legs off a lazy barsted like yourself, bloke.'

'What are you making.'

'A collar for the dog.'

And that, more than anything else, was a declaration that the pup was now with them to stay. He was well again, and his broken ribs healed. Will felt a wild sense of exhilaration in his chest. He had made the right decision to keep the dog and care for him.

'I've still got a bad feeling though, bloke,' said Jim. 'I reckon we'd best make a push in the morning.'

Even Lainey, listening nearby, inclined her head. 'I think we should too.'

***

That second night, when Will was asleep, the little dog heard something disturbing. He left Will's warm swag and listened again to a low rustling sound that bothered him deep in the pit of his gut. He walked to the edge of the firelight and there he saw the dark slithering shape. He started to growl, ominously for such a small dog.

Like all good snake dogs no one needed to teach Little Blue the danger, he knew it instinctively. The mulga snake – some people called them king browns – was as long as a man is tall, with an armoured head and black eyes that missed nothing.

The snake, for her part, smelled the warm bundle of fur and veered closer, as if to investigate a possible food source. Identifying the blue furred creature she stopped, tongue flicking from between her lipless mouth.

Little Blue stood his ground, growling deep in his throat, and when he jumped forward with his jaws open, white milk-teeth bared, he showed something of the fight he would have in his heart every day of his life.

As if knowing that she had met a greater creature, albeit a small one, the snake veered away. There were frogs near the water, and they did not have teeth.

Chapter Nine

Between the Rivers

The three trackers with the police party were from different homelands. Trooper Joseph was Kungkari, from the Barcoo. Trooper Jeremiah was a Pitta Pitta man from around Boulia — they called him the Plains Turkey Man for his long legs and manner of walking with his neck swaying forward and back like that bird. Trooper Matthew was from the coast near Rockhampton, a member of the Darumbal people. In order to communicate amongst themselves they spoke Kriol mixed with some English and the more widely used words of their own tongues.

While Long Douglas enjoyed a long dinner camp the three trackers gathered ahead of the patrol to talk. For two days they had ridden blind, unable to find any spoor made by Will Jones and his crew amongst the hoof marks of many thousands of sheep, making even their significant skills impotent.

Now, however, casting along the edges of the drive, Trooper Matthew had found Will Jones's boot imprinted in the dust, discovering the moment that he and three others deviated from the droving party they had ridden with.

'Here,' he said. 'One man say g'bye an' ride off with them sheep. That outlaw an' his mates they follow the creek bed here, up sunrise way now.'

Trooper Joseph made a face and spat onto the earth. 'I won't go up that Powell Creek. Bad country up there.' He told the others the story of a white man called Welford, who his own Kungkari people had killed. He told how the rest of the tribe had been cornered and slaughtered here by settlers and the Native Police. 'Bad country, sooner ride off home than go there.'

'This Long Douglas from down South,' said Matthew. 'He's a bad man – an' he'll whip us all if we say no to 'im.'

The Kungkari man brightened, 'How about we just take 'im somewhere else?'

'Where?'

Trooper Joseph shrugged and pointed to the Northwest. 'Up that way, between the rivers. Lotsa empty country round there – ride around until he gets plenty tired – pretend we still on the trail.'

The other two men grinned back. It was a good plan.

***

As the three trackers rode back into camp Long Douglas was mounting up with the aid of a handy rock. Settling into the saddle he unclipped the waterbag and took a swig. 'You on the trail yet boys?'

'Yes sir,' said Trooper Joseph. 'Plenty good trail.'

'Well, that's good news anyway. Carry on.'

With the rest of the patrol mounted, they crossed the creek, putting spurs to the horses, charging into the scrub on the other side. The trackers knew how to play the game, finding fictitious 'sign' here and there, and Long Douglas seemed happy enough through the afternoon.

'Look,' Trooper Joseph would say. 'That log is where Will Jones run along, then slide down branch over there.'

Trooper Jeremiah would join in the game. 'Then he hop from rock to rock.'

Picturing these events, Long Douglas would nod his head slowly. 'How far ahead?' he asked, over and over.

'Not far now.'

Slowly they penetrated deeper into a wilderness country between the rivers, but Long Douglas was no fool, and by the middle of the next day he was smelling a rat. 'It doesn't make any sense why they would go Northwest now. Show me some of these tracks,' he demanded. 'Blessed if I've seen any sign for a day or more.'

With no tracks to show, Trooper Joseph changed his story. 'Can't find any more tracks now sergeant. We been casting around, looking.'

Long Douglas's face turned a bright shade of red. 'Well look harder, or starve. No bloody rations for you bastards tonight.' He paused, then approached Benny, the white constable in charge of the Queensland contingent, 'I really must say that I'm in need of a bath and a meal – is there any kind of homestead within an hour or two's ride.'

'Nothing sir,' he said, then grinned. 'Your Lordship might 'ave to go without.'

'Excuse me, you are being insubordinate.'

The constable smirked and walked away.

***

That evening Benny wandered up to the trackers, giving them each a plug of tobacco. They were miserable without tucker, and the baccy helped fill the void. Trooper Jeremiah, who did not burden himself with the paraphernalia of smoking, simply bit off a chunk and chewed it happily.

'I'm jack of this caper,' said the white constable. 'I want to head home. I don't like this Long Douglas fella, this bastard from New South Wales, and neither does anyone else. I got an idea, right?'

When he had finished outlining his proposal the three troopers grinned, and the Kungkari man summed up his feelings for the three of them. 'Plenty good thinking, constable.'

'We've got to do this properly,' said the constable, 'and by tomorrow night we'll be riding home.'

***

When the embers of the fire had burned low, and the stars and moon offered enough light for secret business, the constable rose in the night, taking two men on an erratic night ride, leaving a trail that even Long Douglas would be able to see.

They did just enough anti-tracking to suggest that the trail had been made by fugitives, then returned before dawn for an hour's hard sleep.

After a breakfast of johnny-cakes and tea, Trooper Joseph showed Long Douglas the sign. 'Them bad men not covering their spoor now sir. We follow no trouble now Sergeant.'

***

Yet the going was tough. This was a country of sand, dry channels, gidyea, claypans and spinifex. Long Douglas was in a hurry now, and would brook no delay.

At noon they reached the base of a small hill, and the three troopers climbed to the summit, leaving the remainder of the party down below.

Long Douglas waited until they returned, and Trooper Joseph came to him and hissed. 'I can see Will Jones in his camp from the top sir. Come up and look.'

Scenting victory, Long Douglas unsheathed his Winchester and dismounted, before calling for his field glasses from one of the packs. 'Lead me carefully, Trooper. For I dislike thorns.'

'No thorns,' he was assured, and together the two men set off up the face of the hill, an ancient sandhill hardened to the consistency of stone. At the far side Trooper Joseph insisted that his commander fall prone to the ground, then slither forwards slowly.

'Now look carefully,' said the tracker. 'You'll see his camp in the distance.'

Long Douglas didn't stop to ponder why Trooper Joseph's voice was now behind instead of beside him. Laying the rifle down he picked up the field glasses and began to scan the fore and middle ground, looking for a column of smoke, men, or horses.

At length he said, 'Where are they? I can't see anyone.' He looked around and the tracker was nowhere to be seen. 'Damn your eyes,' he muttered, but he resumed searching through the glasses. A good five minutes passed before he lowered them for the last time, collected the rifle, and got to his feet. 'Damn you, Trooper Joseph, show yourself. What manner of trick is this?'

The trooper had gone.

***

By the time Long Douglas made it down to the base of the hill there was no one there, not even his own horse.

The enormity of the situation he was in: alone in the wilderness with only the six cartridges in the tube magazine of the rifle, and no food or vesta to light a fire, dawned on him.

'Damn you,' he shouted to the sky, but there was no answer, not even an echo.

Chapter Ten

The Fellowship of the Track

With five riding horses, four packs and one dog, the little group rode to the north at a good clip, anxious to leave Long Douglas and his extradition warrant far behind. They kept to bridle tracks along the Barcoo, leaving the main roads to Cobb and Co coaches, bearing travellers and government officials, and honest folk with nothing to fear from the law.

Within a few days Little Blue could walk alongside Will's gelding for most of the day. Tiring by the middle afternoon, Will would lift him up onto his horse, where he would sit forward of the saddle.

After a week or two the pup seemed to gain a mountain of energy. Not only could he match the horses all day, but in camp he became a crazy whirlwind, stealing boots and chewing any unattended object, as well as scavenging from plates left on or near the ground. He also gained a prodigious appetite. Keeping the dog fed became a preoccupation.

'Time to start training that pup,' warned Jim, and Will took up the challenge. Before long Little Blue could sit, drop, and stay. Most of the time.

Travelling at a steady but not hectic pace, keeping clear of drovers and station hands, they camped each night on a suitable waterhole, and ate yellowbelly from the river, caught with Sam's skill on the cat-gut line. Several times Jim retraced their steps to check for pursuit, and found no sign of police on their tail.

Even so, assuming that Long Douglas and his patrol were somewhere behind them, they had decided not to travel openly by their real names. Will introduced himself to the few station workers or travellers they encountered as Thomas; Jim posed as a horse tailer and no one asked his name. Sam pretended to be a Chinese cook.

'I ain't posin' as yer damn wife again,' said Lainey to Will. 'Jest about made me vomit last time I 'ad to do it – down in Eulo before ya got yer stupid self locked up.'

'Well how do we explain a woman ridin' with us then?'

'Simple, I'll pretend to be a bloke.'

Lainey packed her hair up into her hat, borrowed men's clothes from Will, altering them around the waist to fit. She practiced a gruff voice, and became 'Albert.' This was a role she seemed to love playing. She practiced swear words and cultivated phrases like, 'darn you blokes need a good talkin' to wiv me fists,' or 'let's go to town and git us some lassies.'

***

Near Isisford, a settlement they kept a good distance from, they came upon a wagon loaded down with stores, bogged to the bolsters on the far side of a river crossing in a wallow of slick mud. In attendance were two poor station roustabouts, and an overseer with a jumped-up attitude.

'Here you,' he called to Will. 'Get down here and help us.'

'Where did you learn yer manners, mate, a pig-pen?' drawled Will.

'Now you listen to me,' said the overseer. 'I'm from Wakefield Station yonder and I'm overdue with these rations.'

Will dismounted, fixed his horse to a tree branch with the reins, then walked up to the wagon, examined the half-buried wheels, while the two workers took the opportunity to lean on their shovels. The horses in the traces were sweating from the work of trying to haul the load out.

'Best thing, I reckon is to unload the blasted wagon,' said Will. 'Them horses won't have too much trouble draggin' it out then.'

'There's five ton there,' said the overseer. 'We don't have the bloody time.'

'You will if we help out,' said Will. He walked to the wagon and lifted one corner of the tarpaulin cover. He saw sacks of flour, sugar, tea, even some pickled meat in tins. 'We could do with some provisions,' he commented.

'One sack of flour,' said the overseer. 'An' only if you hop to it.'

Will shook his head. 'One bag fer each of us, and some grain for our nags if you've got it. Otherwise we pile on our horses an' ride off.'

'Very well then. One bag each and some feed for your horses.' The overseer spat on his hand and they shook on the deal.

Will, Jim, Sam and 'Albert' worked like dogs to stack the goods on dry ground, with the cover tarp spread beneath to keep out the damp. It was hot work, and the men soon had their shirts off, sweating in the sun, though 'Albert,' for obvious reasons, laboured on fully clothed.

When it seemed that overseer planned to simply supervise the stacking, without lifting a finger himself, Will called out. 'Hey sunshine, what makes you think you've got the right to stand there an' watch?'

With an unhappy grumble the man joined in, while Little Blue sniffed his way around the carthorses, lifted his leg on the wheels, and patrolled the stacked goods as if it was he who was supervising.

They stacked the load high, all five ton of it, and when it was done, and the wagon empty, it didn't take long for the horses to haul the wagon out of the bog.

With the cart free at last, they piled all the stores back on again, with the overseer snapping instructions as to exactly where this or that had to be stowed.

When the wagon rolled on, Will cracked a grin and showed the others a little stash he had made in the scrub beside the bog. As well as the flour bags and a bushel of grain the overseer had given him, Will had five more bags of flour, plenty of sugar and tea, and enough tobacco to last them three months hidden in the grass.

Jim laughed, 'You got nimble hands,' he smiled. 'I never even seen you do that.'

'He were a rude barsted,' said Will. 'I would've taken more, if our packs could've carried it all.'

Chapter Eleven

The Goldfields

Will Jones and his crew travelled on as summer waned into autumn, and the mornings grew cold and crisp as a dry lancewood stick. They followed the Alice River where it swung east near Barcaldine, enduring days of dry country before they camped on the headwaters of the Belyando River, the first easterly drainage they had encountered.

'There's gold around Clermont,' said Will, and their eyes brightened. Even Sam had a spring in his step. They all knew gold and how to win it from the ground. Around the campfire, while Little Blue either rampaged or slept with his chin on his leg, they talked endlessly about snippets they had heard – the names of established fields with enticing names such as The Springs, Venus, McDonald's Flat, and Wild Cat. They talked eagerly about which areas the gold would be reef or alluvial, and reported traveller's verdicts on the current state of the fields.

Fifty miles out from Clermont they passed a couple of miners who told them to avoid the worked-out fields south of the town.

'They're pulling payable gold out at Black Ridge and Miclere,' said one wizened character leading an overloaded mule, his beard as wind-swept and dust-streaked as the bush itself. 'Fifteen mile north of the town. That's where I'd be heading if I were you.'

The following day they reached Miclere, where mullock heaps rose like anthills from the stony earth, headgear abounded, and taciturn men stared daggers at Will and his party as they passed.

Near the middle of the diggings the landscape looked as if it had been turned upside down, with disturbed earth in all directions. All substantial trees had been felled and turned into boards for shoring. Jim reined in his horse, and spat at the ground, a grim expression on his face.

'What's wrong with you?' asked Will.

'Look at it, bloke,' said Jim. 'A damn shame what they done to the land. You fellas can stay here if you want. I'm goin' back to where every blade a' grass hasn't been torn out.'

'Ain't ya never seen a gold diggin's before?' asked Will.

'Not like this,' said Jim.

'Well you shoulda been at the Turon,' said Will, 'it was worse than this fer fifty miles. Come on mate, let's at least get a peek at the town.'

Jim shook his head. 'I don't like it, bloke. No respect for country.'

Will sighed and looked at Lainey who shrugged, then Sam.

'If Jim wanna go back to find good camp I ride with him,' said Sam.

'We'll all go,' said Will, turning his horse. 'But it's a two-mile ride back to country that's anything like natural.'

In fact, it was nearer three miles before they found a half-decent waterhole in Miclere Creek. Even here there were piles of spoil, some up to six feet high, and abandoned shafts to match, but there were plenty of trees, grass for the horses, and the creek was stunning. Little Blue approved of the site straight off, and fetched himself into the water for a dip, heading back into camp to shake all over Lainey, who chased him out of the camp. All of this was great fun to the pup, and he set off to repeat the process.

Once they'd set up camp Will was restless, unable to settle. 'I've a taste for a beer,' he declared. 'An' it should be safe enough. There's no way in hell Long Douglas will have chased us this far north, and even he ain't enough to stop me from slakin' me thirst.'

Sam regarded Will gravely, with his arms folded in front of his chest. 'Remember what bad thing happen last time you went drinkin',' he said.

'Ah good Jesus I hate you barsteds with long memories. There'll be no lock-up for me this time, I guarantee it. You want to come, Jim?'

'Back into that wasteland? No thanks, bloke. I'll stop here an' help Sam and the dog watch the horses. If ya wanna bring us back a bottle or two I'd be grateful, but.'

'I'll go with you,' said Lainey, 'but as I said before, I aren't playin' your wife.' She balled her fists. 'Me name's Albert and no cove better give me any lip or I'll fight him there and then.'

The others laughed at her pluck, and soon went about their business. By the time Will and Lainey had washed, dressed and mounted up, Fat Sam already had the small gold pan out and was heading down to a gravel bank, with Little Blue wandering along excitedly at this new game. Will used his heels to ease his gelding into a trot, a little nervous about the excursion, but comforted by the Webley revolver in the holster at his side.

Back in Miclere the main street was a swathe of hoof prints and piles of dung. There were a couple of stores, just shanties really – a store, and an eatery that doubled as a sly grog shop on the creek.

Lainey, her hair beneath her hat, walked in with Will, heading for the bar – a long slab of yellow messmate, sawn by giants with crosscut saws. Will reached out to trace the pattern of the grain, the story told by that old tree.

He ordered two pots of ale, and the roast meal on offer, then explained, 'Me an' a couple of mates are looking to make a dollar or two here. 'Ow does a bloke get a foothold in this place?'

The shanty owner looked like an old military man, complete with a handlebar moustache, waxed and twisted at the ends. 'Depends if you 'as capital or not.'

'Very little capital mate, just strong backs.'

'Just about everything payable 'as been pegged and worked already. There's some big players 'ere though, and they're always looking for labourers—ten bob a week an' all found or near enough. One of 'em is working the reef we call the "Deep Lead." Everyone who's tried before has been beaten by water over the basalt, but these blokes are through it now, working payable wash 128 feet down. That's the deepest mine in Queensland,' he added proudly.

Will passed a shilling coin and took his change, surprised at having just bought the most expensive drink of his life, then accepted the two pots of ale, passing one to Lainey.

They took a seat outside, and Will noticed that at an adjacent table sat a man with a silk tie and jacket, nursing what looked like rum and water in a glass. Will grunted 'G'day,' at him, then turned to Lainey. 'I don't fancy the notion of labourin' fer some damned company; workin' ourselves to the bone. Swingin' a pick and pushin' barrows a hundred feet underground fer two pounds a month ain't my cup of tea.' He looked at Lainey. 'Maybe we should head back to sheep an' cattle country – find ourselves a station job.'

Lainey shook her head, a line of froth from the ale like a high tide mark on her upper lip. 'We come here to find gold. I reckon that's what we should do. Sam's a clever prospector, you told me that yerself. It's just a matter headin' up and down the creeks until we find somethin' payable, isn't it?'

Will shrugged, 'This area has been worked for a good number of years. There would have been prospectors combing the area all that time. We'll need to be lucky to find what they missed.'

They fell silent for a while, and Will went up to the bar and returned with a second round. 'It's a costly ale,' he said as he steadily lowered the level. 'But I don't reckon I've ever had better.' By the third drink they had also collected plates of roast mutton, potatoes and gravy, and were attacking it ravenously.

A commotion from inside made Will break off eating, and they both looked as a wiry digger staggered through, holding a tankard by the handle. His drunken eyes focussed on Lainey.

'Oi, mate!' he said. 'Take yer hat off when yer eating.'

Lainey looked up at him. 'What's it got to do with you?'

'I jes know bad manners when I see 'em. Take your hat off!'

Lainey put on her huskiest voice, and stood up. 'Well I appreciate your thoughts, but if you don't piss off it'll be the worse for ya.'

The drunk stopped, swaying on his feet, staring at Lainey, 'Well ain't you a fresh-faced young feller? Scarcely ever seen a razor that face has. Is that what you gotta wear a hat for, to keep your skin pretty?'

The man in the silk tie at the adjacent table suddenly rose from his seat, a shilling coin in his hand. 'Here son,' he said in a deep voice. 'Take this and go buy another drink.'

The man's eyes fell on the coin. He took it, then looked back at the giver. 'That young feller should take 'is damn hat off. E needs to be taught manners.'

'Just go and have a drink,' said the man. 'There's a good fellow.'

With a last look at Lainey, the drunk wandered off towards the bar.

Will turned, 'That was good of you, mate. Thanks muchly, though I don't reckon that bloke was worth a shilling. Albert here was about to knock 'is block off fer free.'

The man simply inclined his head, and continued to sit there, keeping his own company while Lainey and Will finished their meal and another pot of ale.

'That drunken cow is still inside there,' said Will. 'Keeps looking out and muttering to some of his mates. Maybe we'd better head back to camp.'

After purchasing a couple of bottles of beer and securing them in their saddle bags, they mounted up, and rode through town, watching the mining camps segueing from day business to that of the night, parties of rowdy diggers just beginning their carousing. Two horsemen raced neck and neck along the track so fast that Will and Lainey had to ride out of the way, their whooping and carrying on making the horses skittish.

'Crazy place,' said Lainey.

They were just riding through the outskirts of the town when they looked back to see that the man in the silk tie was fifty yards behind them, mounted on a handsome bay thoroughbred.

'He trailin' us, do you reckon?' Lainey asked.

'Dunno yet.'

But as they left town, and diverted down and around a few mullock heaps, the man remained doggedly on their trail.

Will loosened his squirt in its holster. 'He's playin' a dangerous game, but I've got no intention of leadin' the barsted to our camp. Let's stop an' see what he wants.'

The two of them drew into the side of the track and waited. The man with the silk tie continued to ride towards them at a slow amble. Will drew his weapon, broke it to check the load, then held it loosely across his knees.

At a distance of perhaps ten paces the other man stopped his mount.

'Who are you?' called Will. 'An' what the hell do you mean by follerin' us around?'

Chapter Twelve

The Offer

The man with the silk tie walked his horse up close, and his steely eyes never deviated from Will's, ignoring the revolver that was aimed directly at his gut. He sat ramrod straight in what looked like an English hunting saddle, and the stub of a cigar, unlit, protruded from the corner of his lips.

'Stop right there, mister,' said Will. 'I don't care who y'are, I'll ruin yer day if you come any closer.'

At this the silk tie man reined in at last, plucked the cigar from his mouth and inclined his head. 'Forgive me for following you in the dark, sir, and I can understand your misapprehension. Allow me to introduce myself, my name is Henry Sutton, formerly of London Town. I simply wish to talk to you. That's all. I've got a proposal that you might find interesting, and of great profit to us both.'

'I don't like strangers much,' said Will, still not lowering his weapon, 'an' you're a strange stranger if ever I met one, with yer fancy duds and posh talk.'

'Give me ten minutes of your time, that's all. If you don't like what you hear I'll ride off and never bother you again.' Seeing that Will was still hesitating he opened his jacket wide to show that he carried no knife or gun. 'I am unarmed and bear you no malice. I will be at your mercy.'

Will looked at Lainey, who shrugged and said, 'Can't hurt to listen.'

With a final scowl Will holstered the revolver. 'Alright then, come back to camp, but stay behind me an' ride slow or ya might cop a bullet from our mates – they're trigger happy cows and no mistake.'

'You won't regret this,' said the man, and when they set off he was careful to stay behind Lainey and Will, who rode abreast, through a long ride in the dark to the creek-side camp.

As they approached the spot Will called ahead to Sam and Jim, and they came out of the firelight, both armed and on edge. Little Blue trotted beside Jim, and, having seen the visitor, his tail was up high, almost rigid, and his ears lying flat. A low growl emanated from deep in the back on his throat.

'Boys,' said Will. 'This cove 'ere is called Henry Sutton, an' he's keen to tell us about some proposal or other he's cooked up. I've promised him our ears for a bit, then he'll ride away – he's unarmed, so no need fer weapons.'

Neither Sam nor Jim looked impressed, but they both helped to sort the horses. It was Little Blue, however, who took the dimmest view of their guest. He sat as far away as he could, while still being within the firelight, and continued to growl softly until Will told him to stop.

Henry Sutton, meanwhile, settled down before the fire with a new cigar burning. Will lit his pipe and passed a quart pot of tea around. Jim and Sam shared one of the bottles of beer Will had brought back, pouring it into frothy mugs and drinking heartily.

For the first quarter hour or more Will picked the stranger's brains about the goldfields from Clermont north to Charters Towers. He wanted to know how many people were making money, and how many weren't. He wanted to know the weights of some recent nuggets and areas to avoid. For Sam's benefit he asked where on the fields they might find Cantonese Chinese – Sam's own people of whom he was in fear of his life.

For all his posh ways the stranger knew the area well, and had obviously made a close study of other men's business. He spent much more than the agreed ten minutes – twice that amount of time – in summarising the Central Queensland goldfields – including where the Wardens were located and what kind of men they were.

Finally, Will said, 'So now, what's this proposal you want to talk to us about?'

'Well,' said the stranger, who paused to cough into a handkerchief. 'Some partners and I have a small mining company of our own, and we've recently started working a new field to the north-west of here, in the Lyver Range. We've got five claims running there ourselves plus half a dozen independents. We've just installed a steam powered battery. I'm looking for more parties to work claims and bring the ore to my plant for crushing.'

Will saw that both Jim and Sam were listening intently, and there was barely a sound but for the crackling of the fire and a distant curlew. 'Go on,' he said.

'The idea is simple. I give you a claim to register in your name – all pegged out and ready. You work the claim and bring your ore to the company battery, and I process it and pay cash for the gold.'

'Why?'

'Simply because I'm running my own mines, but I need more diggers in the area to make the machinery pay its way.'

'Why not just employ more men and work the claims yourself?'

'Under the terms of the Goldfields Act the Warden has already granted us the maximum number of claims we can work – the original claim plus four more. We could go bigger but we have to jump through a fair number of hoops in order to do so. That's why I'm looking for people to register their own claims on the field.'

'How much gold?'

'Most of the claims are running three to five ounces to the ton along the seam.'

Fat Sam whistled and grinned, his long-stemmed pipe in his hand.

'It sounds too good to be true,' said Will. 'Why us?'

'I've been looking out for groups like you – new to the area. Hardworking folk keen on a piece of the action but with no real capital to speak of.'

Will said nothing. His share of the hundred pounds from the Kyungra Station affair was sewn up in his swag. 'I'll tell you what. We'd like to have a look around Miclere and Black Ridge fer a day or two – it's been a long journey an' we need to plan our next move. We'll talk about it, an' might ride up for a look later in the week, fair enough?'

'Very fair indeed,' Sutton said, and he passed across a pamphlet titled, Miners Wanted. 'This will give you more information, and there's a map on the inside.'

'Here,' said Will, taking the pamphlet. 'I'll get your nag for ya, and thanks for the chin-wag, I learned a lot. Might see you soon an' we might not. See what 'appens.'

The stranger smiled and made his farewells to each of them in turn, before mounting up and riding out into the night.

After Henry Sutton rode away he stopped down the road and reached behind him for the tiny derringer pistol that he'd stuck in the back of his waistband. It was getting quite uncomfortable by then. He was pleased that he hadn't needed to use the weapon. It seemed certain to him that Will Jones and his mates would do what he wanted without any need for violence.

Chapter Thirteen

Jim Rides Home

For the next three days Sam wandered the banks, flats and gullies of Miclere Creek with Jim, panning old mullock heaps or digging fresh gravel samples from likely patches on the creek. Will wore his gelding flat learning the lay of the land; looking at claims for sale and getting a grasp of the extent of the diggings.

Lainey, meanwhile, became mates with a woman digging a claim with her husband half a mile away, a sassy young Irishwoman called Bridget, and she was often in the camp, drinking rum and carrying on, a couple of ankle-biters terrorising the pup until he learned to hide when he saw them coming.

In the evenings Jim was silent and morose, not quite himself, and though Will tried to jolly him up, he seemed disinclined to respond with his usual wit.

'Watch out ya don't trip over on your own lip, mate,' Will called. 'It aren't like you to look so down.'

'There ain't too much to be smilin' about, bloke,' said Jim. 'I liked it better back home, before you decided we had to take Clarkie's letter halfway across the country, an' you got pegged for 'is murder.'

'I didn't see you complainin' when we split the hunnerd pounds.'

Jim shrugged, 'The money was good, but I'd rather be home.'

Will narrowed his eyes, 'You got a woman down there, is that it?'

Lainey was protective of their comrade. 'Maybe he has,' she said. 'At least it would be a real woman, not just a picher on a post card like the one that you stare at every night.'

'I don't look at her every night, and shut yer gob anyway – she's none of your damn business.'

Lainey's hands were on her hip, by now, 'Well just leave Jim alone. Everybody's allowed their own feelin's, Will.'

Most of the conversation in and around the camp centred on their next move as a group. Staying put was one possibility – Sam was finding small flakes in the wash, just a few drams all up – but in time they might find richer ground worth pegging. Buying a working claim with payable gold, Will had found out, was out of their price range.

The general agreement seemed to be that they would soon ride north to investigate Henry Sutton's new field, though it wasn't until the third evening at the camp that they discussed it in detail. It was Sam's opinion that checking out the Sutton claims was worth the ride. Lainey was happy to move on and give the plan a go.

'We're resolved then,' said Will, taking Jim's silence as agreement. 'We'll ride up and have a look at this new field of Henry Sutton's.'

'Not me,' said Jim. 'I'm goin' off, for a bit.'

The declaration was like a charge of powder going off in the middle of the camp. Even Sam looked stunned. A long silence ensued, until finally Will gathered the wit to speak. 'You aren't coming wif us? What the devil do you mean by that? Are you plannin' on stoppin' here by yerself?'

'Nah mate. I mean that I'm ridin' away fer a spell. I ain't ready fer diggin' holes and pickin' through dirt right now.'

'What are you going to do then?'

'I'm gonna head south. I need to see my people—my own country.'

'You're going to ride all the way back past the border?' Will knew that Jim's homelands were centred on the plains around the town of Coonamble, east to the banks of Teridgerie Creek where he had been born.

Jim inclined his head, 'Yes, bloke. That's what I have to do – see my people – spend some time on my country. I figure that on my way down I can find out whether Long Douglas is still on our trail, or if he's given up.'

Lainey busily making tea, gave a little groan, 'Oh c'mon Jim. I hate us to split up. Give it three months, an' if it ain't worked for us then we'll all give up on it.'

'No. I've made up me mind. I'll pack up tonight and ride away at dawn.'

Will turned on Sam, 'You ain't saying much there.'

It was always hard to read much on the Cantonese man's rounded face, but when he shrugged it seemed to take an effort. He and Jim were best of mates and thick as thieves. It would be a hard separation for Sam. 'Jim do what he reckons 'e needs to fo,' was all he said.

'Well it's a bit of hard luck for us,' said Will. 'Now we're a man short for working a claim, when we finally get one. But yes, it would be worthwhile knowing what's goin' on with Long Douglas.'

***

The next morning, a wedge-tailed eagle, flying high in the morning sun, catching the early thermals over the hard dirt of the diggings, saw one man ride away from the camp, heading south, trailing a roan pack horse. The man looked good in the saddle, as competent a rider and bushman as any of his kind.

Holding his station, the eagle watched the man's former companions breaking camp and heading north, with a dog, spare horses and packs.

If the eagle wondered why the fellowship had broken up he gave no sign, just saw the lone rider look up and find him in the sky, lifting his left hand in a wave of silent companionship.

Men like Jim are never alone in the bush.

Chapter Fourteen

Faith, Hope and the Prodigal

Will, Lainey and Sam rode to the north-west on the Charters Towers track, then veered off, following the map on the brochure Henry Sutton had given them. Little Blue ran alongside, straying now and then to investigate the scent of wallaby or dingo until a sharp whistle from Will brought him back.

By and by they saw less mining activity along the track, though prospectors could be seen working in and along the creek beds, while drovers and their dogs flanked herds of sheep or cattle strung for a mile or more along the tracks and winding creeks, wheeling unruly bullocks; whips cracking against the blue sky. Watching them, Will felt a pang for the simple hardships and pleasures of stock work, and when he locked eyes with Sam he saw that he was watching them too.

'I reckon Little Blue will make a good working dog, when the chance arises,' Will said. 'I'd like to try him out one day.'

'When we're rich from the diggings,' said Lainey, 'you can buy yer own place an' Little Blue can chase sheep or cattle 'round as much a 'e sees fit.'

Will grinned, and the thought kept him warm through noon and the early afternoon, at which time they passed a small township with a pub and store, then arrived at the top of a rise. From there they looked upon Henry Sutton's goldfield, spread out across a set of further hills and their valleys. The three riders reined in and studied the area without a word, and Will's practiced eye was already summing up the opportunities presented below.

The diggings were scattered around the hills, with some substantial buildings in the centre of the first valley. Dark smoke trailed from the stack of a stationary steam engine, and the clatter of the ore battery carried on the warm air. There was activity at every turn—men, horses, wagons. Mine headgear bristled from more than a dozen sites.

'Looks busy,' grunted Will.

'Surely does,' agreed Lainey.

Sam said nothing. He had his pipe going by then, taking in smoke at a furious pace.

'Does it look like gold-bearing country to you Sam?' Will asked.

Sam shrugged, 'Not very well certain just now.' But he pointed to the broken ground on which their horses stood, sharp with feldspar, and the glint of galena. There was no doubt this was a highly mineralised area.

A couple of men near the battery seemed to spot them, one pointing up with an extended arm.

'Should we ride down?' asked Lainey.

'I don't reckon we have to,' replied Will. 'Looks like Sutton himself saddling up down there.'

This observation turned out to be correct, for the Englishman was soon taking the slope at a canter towards them, finally reining in and walking up close enough to shake Will's hand, and remove his hat to greet Lainey.

The formalities done, Sutton turned his horse to take in the view. 'I'm glad we're up here, for it gives me a chance to explain the geology of the field.' He pointed the stub of a cigar down to the valley. 'The parent rock — through these hills - is a granodiorite, containing feldspar, and through it winds fault-fissures of gold-bearing quartz. There are three of these leaders, and we call them Faith, Hope and the Prodigal. Sometimes they are just a few inches wide, sometimes four or five feet. The best thing is that they are close to the surface, often only ten or twelve feet, but varying down to thirty. There's also some alluvial gold in the gullies.'

'So what are you offering us?' asked Will.

'I've got some choices for you – claims that can potentially access one or other of the gold leaders. We'll ride the area and you can decide.' He paused. 'What happened to the other fellow?'

'Jim had to ride south, means we're shorthanded but …'

'One of my own men is looking to start mining for himself and is looking for partners. I'll introduce you later – you might be able to work something out with him. Now, are you ready for a tour?'

'We are,' said Will. 'Please lead on.'

For the next hour and a half, they rode with Sutton, starting with the company leases, all neatly pegged and headgear built in solid fashion. They shook hands with overseers and engineers, and viewed some half dozen leases that were pegged and ready for registration.

They stopped to talk to several other sets of battlers working leases.

'We ain't getting' rich,' was the general refrain, 'but we're making steady money, and hoping for the good patches.'

Will was impressed. Most fields had big winners and big losers. This one seemed to be producing consistently. Of the three gold leaders, it seemed that Faith was the most consistent but unspectacular in terms of return, Hope was less reliable but very rich in places, while the Prodigal was frustratingly hard to find, often petering out completely, but yielded incredible gold returns in places.

Henry Sutton smiled sagely when Will made his observations, 'It's a good field — no one is riding around in golden carriages, but there's money for all, and the halcyon days are still to come.'

Finally, with the horses being cared for by one of Sutton's men, they toured the stamp battery on foot. Here the gold ore was machine-crushed to access the yellow metal hidden in the quartz. This monster was powered by a Robey steam engine, the main cylinder shaft shining with chrome as it cycled, the eccentric working the slide valve with a huff and snort of steam.

Out the front of the engine house was a terrier cross, of unknown ancestry — a haughty, superior kind of dog – short haired and scarred around the neck. Will paid the animal scarcely any mind – he was more interested in the battery - its eight stamps working furiously in turn to crush the ore to a powder.

The final, and most interesting shed was where a slurry of crushed ore was mixed with mercury, which then dissolved the gold therein. The mercury was removed from the mix and boiled away, leaving gold in its natural state. These pellets of near-pure gold were an intoxicating sight, and a man sat watchfully near the door, with a carbine over his knees.

Outside the building Will shook Sutton's hand. 'I'm impressed with the capital you an' yer partners have poured in here.'

'We've spent a pretty penny getting this place set up,' agreed Sutton. 'We've done everything right, so far. Now what's your thoughts? Do you want to be a part of it or not?'

Will scraped at the stubble on his chin between his thumb and forefinger. 'We'll camp the night by the claims you suggested. We'll wash a panful or two from the creeks around and talk amongst ourselves. You'll have an answer tomorrow.'

Just then there was a shout and that garbled, barking, growling snarl of two dogs in combat. It was Lainey's cry that made Will realise that one member of the whirling fight, enfolded in a swirl of dust, was Little Blue, and the other was the terrier from near the doorway.

Lainey turned to him, terrified, 'Stop 'em Will.'

It was obvious that Little Blue was getting the worst of it, but he was scrapping bravely against a much bigger and more experienced opponent.

A man had appeared from inside, arms folded over his chest.

'Is that your dog?' asked Will.

'Yeah, that's my Rossie.'

'Well call him off.'

'Well I would, but he won't listen anyhow.'

Will swore and hurried into the fray, trying to grab Little Blue's tail, but it was moving way too fast. He diverted off to the side and grabbed a thin, straight branch, fallen from a gum tree. He looked up at the other man.

The terrier had a hold on Little Blue's throat, still on the loose ruff, but he was improving his grip. Little Blue was yelping now, becoming more muffled as time went on.

'I'm going to hit your dog,' Will said, and he swung the stick as hard as he could into the terrier's rump. The blow did the trick. The animal released Little Blue and scampered away from the fight to the nearby shadows.

Lainey was at Little Blue's side in a moment. 'Oh you poor thing,' she said.

'You ever hit my dog again and I'll hit you,' said the man.

Will was in no mood for threats. 'I can't see any point waiting,' he said. 'You want to fight let's do it now.'

Henry Sutton came striding out from inside. 'There'll be no fighting. Get back to work Johnson, and if I see that dog off a chain again I'll shoot him.'

Will was disappointed, but he slowly relaxed as the other man walked back into the factory, stopping only to tie his dog, smirking at Will as he went.

'I hope this little incident won't affect your decision of whether to stay or not.' the Englishman said.

Will kneeled and clapped to bring Little Blue to him. The pup had a streak of blood on his muzzle. 'Not at all,' he said. 'I ain't ever run from trouble, and I won't start now.'

Chapter Fifteen

The Blue Dog Mine

'Ain't never run from trouble?' Lainey said laughingly that evening at their camp. 'Not long ago I seen you run from New South Wales with half the traps in the state after yer ... and then there was that time when ...'

'That's different,' said Will.

'How?'

'Even Ned Kelly bolted from the traps when he had to.'

'Not at Glenrowan, he didn't. Or Ben Hall – now he were a man who faced up to things.'

'Well, it did him a lot of good, being six feet under and full of lead, like he is.'

Will was watching Sam panning through a shovel full of gravel he had gleaned from one of the gullies. He was near the last wash now, and Will leaned closer to see the small 'tail' of gold that remained. 'Just a few specks, but it's the real thing,' he declared.

Sam set about removing the gold dust he had panned with the tip of his finger, transferring each grain to a glass bottle filled with water.

'That's hardly a fortune,' said Lainey.

Sam pointed at the ground, 'Down there is real gold. The gully just where it washed out.' He paused, put down the pan and wiped his brow with his sleeve.

'If we stay here,' said Will. 'We have to decide on a claim, and to do that we have to choose which of the three quartz leaders we want to mine.'

They'd all heard Henry Sutton explain the nature of the three leaders – nice safe Faith, which should allow them to earn a living, the possibly more lucrative Hope, and the frustrating, elusive Prodigal, with it's potential for big money — or total failure.

'I vote for the Prodigal,' said Lainey. 'I ain't here to grub a living – if there's a chance of striking it rich I want to take it.'

'I'm thinkin' along the same lines as you,' said Will. 'Sam?'

The Cantonese put the pan down, came to his feet and inclined his head. 'Me too. The Prodigal,' he said. He looked in the direction of the most western of the three hills, where the claims mining that more elusive reef were located. There were four or five available. 'Shame Jim not here with us.'

'Yeah, it'd be good to have the barsted along on this lark,' agreed Will, 'even just to hold a shovel and look like e's busy. He'll be back directly, and we'll be rich enough to ride off with him. So which of those claims do you reckon will pay?'

Sam exhaled and wrapped his arms around his middle. 'Sometime quartz reef get richer as she backs into the harder ground on the hill—that banatite layer fold up there, maybe. Furthest of them claims our best chance.'

'Then let's register the damn thing an' get to work – we're only risking the five-pound fee, an' a bit of shoring timber and what-not. When all's said and done if we find nothing worth finding we can move on.' Will grimaced, 'But are you two really up for digging a shaft – we're in for months of hellish work?'

Sam made a face, as if the question had insulted his dignity. 'We need one more man.'

'That we do. I wonder who this cove is that Sutton has in mind for us.'

***

The next morning Will rode up to the battery office to talk to Henry Sutton. They shook hands on the claim that Sam had decided on.

'Welcome to our little enterprise,' Sutton said. 'I've got some good news too. I've had word that the Mine Warden will be out here tomorrow – that'll save you a ride to Clermont to register the claim.'

'That's good news,' said Will. 'Means we can get stuck into things straight off.' He paused. 'Now you mentioned that you had a bloke here who's looking for partners. We could do with an extra pair of hands.'

'I did,' said Sutton. 'You actually met him yesterday.'

Will scratched his head, 'Not the bloke with that blasted dog?'

'Yes, Johnson, that's him – you two didn't get off to a good start, but he's a regular good fellow and just the kind you'll want beside you when the going's hard. He's been labouring here at the plant for the last month or two – he's a better-than-average stoker so I know he's good with a shovel and doesn't mind heavy labour. Here, I'll bring him in.'

Sutton left and returned a few minutes later with Johnson, who sat down, his feet leaving prints of dust across the office floorboards. Now that Will had time to look at the man he noted that he had a stiff moustache, the rest of his face stubbled with whiskers, and piercing eyes.

'I dunno if me dog would appreciate us taking you on as a partner,' Will said.

'Well, I gen'rally make decisions for meself,' said the man. 'An' leave the dog out of it.'

Will cogitated on that for a moment then, 'Where ya from, anyway?'

'Dairy country on the Manning River down New South Wales. Missus started messin' around with me brother who I shared the farm with an' I walked out.' He paused and looked down, then felt in his pocket for his pipe. 'I have to admit that I know next to nothin' about mining, but I know how to work.'

'Dairy farmers generally do,' said Will, feeling more kindly disposed towards the man. He went on to explain the location of the claim that he, Sam and Lainey had decided on.

Johnson agreed. 'Sounds like the right caper to me. I'll either make good money or move on. No point bustin' a gut for no reason.'

Sutton said, 'I'm happy for Alec to keep on bunking down over here, rather than having to camp on site, and he can leave his dog chained up here, at least at first. That'll forestall any problems.'

Will clamped his lips together in a resolute line. 'Right then – we'll give it a go. You, me, Lainey and Sam, split the work and go quarter shares in the payouts, fair enough?'

Johnson lifted an eyebrow, 'One of the four is a woman, is she gonna earn a full share?'

'Oh yes, she will. Lainey's me sister, if she aren't down the shaft doin' a full shift she'll be pullin' her weight one way or another.'

'Orright then, sounds like a deal.'

They shook on it.

'Wander over when you're ready,' said Will, 'and we'll start working out how we're goin' to approach this. Meanwhile we'll move camp over to the claim.'

'What are you going to call your mine?' asked Sutton.

'Oh, Lainey's already decided on that,' Will said. 'It's going to be called the Blue Dog Mine.' He looked at Johnson quizzically. The name was a kind of declaration as to who the senior partners were in this enterprise. 'Is that alright with you.'

'I don't care what we call the blasted thing as long as we pull gold out of it,' he said.

Before Will left, Henry Sutton produced a contract for him to sign. It was a simple enough document. It stipulated that Will and his partners agreed that all ore produced by the mine would be processed by the battery. More unusually, however, it went on to set a minimum of ten ton of ore per working week.

Will frowned, reading through the clause. 'Ten ton minimum? What if we're not on the leader yet, and just bringing out dross?'

Sutton lifted a quill from a holder, inked it, and held it out for Will. 'We've found that there are small amounts of gold all through the substrate, and we like to have the battery going – keeps the men and machinery busy. The ten ton minimum is mainly to stop people speculating on these claims – we want working, productive mines here wherever possible.

Will signed the contract – ten ton wasn't that much, after all – then walked back to their camp. As he passed by the busy little mines of the field he started to wonder why it all seemed to be a little too easy, but then he dismissed the thought from his mind.

That night he dreamed of gold ingots, piled high in the middle of their camp. He was riding a thoroughbred that might have graced the Brisbane Cup. Beside him walked the girl in the post card, dressed in a silk dress of pure white.

Chapter Sixteen

Jim and Long Douglas

Gamilaroi Jim rode south and west, retracing his previous journey with Will, Lainey and Sam along the Alice and the Barcoo. Most often he found a glade along the river to camp through the afternoon, then set off again by night and rode until noon the next day. The coastal route would have been faster, but there were more people, smaller farms and he had promised Will that he would investigate whether Long Douglas and his men were still on his trail.

Near Blackall Jim's roan mare became reluctant to trot, and she developed a strange roll to her walk. The cause, Jim found, was an abscess in the offside front hoof, and he could not afford the time to rest her.

Instead, with a caressing hand on her neck, he thanked her for the many miles they had covered together, then released her into a dark Mulgrave Station horse paddock, roping a buckskin stallion in return. It was a victimless crime, he reckoned, for the two horses were roughly comparable in quality, and the mare would recover.

Riding onwards in the night, Jim enjoyed the wildness of the stallion, edgy and energetic; pig-rooting a couple of times in the first few hours, once stopping dead and stubbornly dropping his head to feed. When Jim let him run, however, the stallion had a turn of speed that was both exhilarating and a little dangerous.

By sunrise, when Jim stopped to brush his new mount, boil the billy and make johnny cakes on the coals they both knew who was boss, and the horse had a name – Cartridge. While Jim ate, the stallion made a nuisance of himself with the packhorse, a ten-year-old mare who wanted nothing to do with his youthful ways, and Jim had to separate them with different lead ropes.

The station brand on Jim's new mount didn't bother him too much – he didn't intend on visiting towns until he reached the New South Wales border in any case. Jim could see or hear other parties moving through the bush from a great distance, and it was rare that he was spotted when he did not want to be.

Past Diamond Downs, on the Barcoo, Jim decided that he would take a few days off the track to follow up what had happened to the police patrol that had followed them. To this end he set off on a short cut through the back-blocks of Albilbah Station and Gilgunyah.

After a day's hard ride, in light scrub on orange dirt, Jim cut the track of a man, barefooted and with a heavy limp. He dismounted to study the spoor up close, noting the marks on the ground made by a stick the man had used to walk with. The tracks were several weeks old.

Jim began to follow, and it was soon obvious that the man was lost, stumbling in great, wide circles through this vast and mostly uninhabited land. The tracks took him into rough country – a range that was marked on Jim's map as the Strathconan Highlands.

Over the next twelve hours Jim found campsites, some scattered with wallaby bones. He found a spent brass case lying on the earth where it had been discarded. The man was armed and able to shoot meat, it seemed.

Forced to camp by the darkness of a new moon, Jim was back in the saddle early, and now the sign changed – lots of comings and goings – as if the man he was following had taken up residence in this area. He found the sites of several more kills.

Finally, he rode towards a rocky peak, jagged with plates of hard rock, with outstretched wings like buttress roots and an overhanging ledge deep in the lee. Jim's sensitive nose picked up the scent of a campfire, and he dismounted and walked in.

There, beside a hearth of dead coals was a heavily bearded man dressed in tattered clothing, close to death it seemed, though he sat up and coughed, saw Jim and tried to run – before falling back to the ground. One of his legs was swollen and red and the very air smelled of putrefaction.

There was a rifle beside the man but he made no effort to pick it up. Jim guessed that he was out of cartridges.

It was the remnants of the clothing that gave the man's identity away to Jim, then the face became visible amongst the grime and dirt. Yet it was a terrified face, for he also had recognised his visitor.

'Inspector Douglas,' said Jim. 'What happen to you, bloke?'

'Get away from me,' said Long Douglas.

'You're gonna die if I leave you here, an' I ain't about to do that.'

'They left me,' said Long Douglas. 'They left me in the bush to die. Murdering curs. I'll have them dismissed from the force … horse-whipped.'

'You ain't gonna do anything 'cept for letting me take a look at that leg,' said Jim. 'Right now I ain't yer enemy, bloke – I'm yer best mate.'

Chapter Seventeen

A Lonely Grave

'I won't be ministered to by a damn outlaw,' spat Long Douglas.

Jim knelt beside him in any case. The policeman's left leg had obviously been broken – and badly – it was swollen to twice the size of the other. The scent of gangrene was deep, like old cheese, and the extent of this murderous flesh-rot showed in the angry stripes that wound around the leg, visible through the ragged strips of his breeches.

'Don't touch it,' warned Long Douglas.

'Orright then,' said Jim. 'If you'd rather I'll cook us a feed and brew some tea.'

While Jim gathered sticks and built the fire, Long Douglas lolled back and seemed to doze. It was dark before he stirred again, at which point he raised his head, ate some fresh johnny-cake and sipped at a quart pot of tea. All the while droplets of sweat flowed down his forehead, and Jim could only imagine the fever that raged inside the sick man's head.

'Can you tell me what happened, bloke?'

Long Douglas's eyes rolled back like marbles, and there was a pause before he began to speak. 'Like I said before, those cursed Queensland troopers took my horse and stole away like thieves. They didn't like me from the start.'

'But that don't explain the leg?'

'After they abandoned me I walked for three days. At a dirty little waterhole – just a puddle really – I came upon a small herd of brumbies. Most of the mob ran, but one was interested – a bay mare of about fourteen hands with a snow-white blaze. When the others shied she came a little way towards me. I could see her brand and the scars of old saddle-galls. I sweet talked her for an hour before I got close. There was no doubt in my mind that she had once been a riding horse but God alone knew for how long she had been running wild.' Long Douglas paused to hold his head between the flat of both hands as if squeezing the memories out. Then he went on; 'I had no rope for a halter, and no other tack at all, so my only chance was to try to get on her back and tame her – stay on until I reached a station or town – even a damned track or fence line.

'Finally she let me rub her neck, and with a light grip on her mane I steered her towards uneven ground where I'd have a chance of mounting up. As you know I am not a tall man. I had only my rifle slung on my back so I had nothing to impede me.'

'It was a good plan, bloke,' Jim commented, 'an' you done well to get up close to her.'

'When we reached the rocky ground I took my opportunity, found a handy clump and clambered aboard. Well,' he tried to laugh but it came out as a wheeze. 'I knew she was going to buck but not how. She knew every trick in the New South Wales Mounted Police horsemanship manual, and then some. In no time at all I was on the ground and my leg broken below the knee.' He sighed deeply. Almost a wail. 'I was a proud man once, but everything just got worse … and worse. Too many weeks to count of pain … oh I learned to sit with the rifle for hour after hour 'til a kangaroo happened along, but the bullets are all gone now, and my only rescuer is a dammed outlaw … and he came too late.'

Jim shook his head sadly. 'Will you let me look at the leg now?'

Long Douglas shook his head, 'If you'd come along a week ago something might have been done, but I'm finished now – even taking my leg won't help.'

Jim saw no reason to contradict him. The disease had progressed too far for even drastic measures. There were however, things he would like to know from Long Douglas, and now seemed as good a time as any to ask them.

Jim cleared his throat, 'You know that Will Jones never murdered anyone, don't you bloke? Clarkie was dead in the saddle when he rode into our camp on the Castlereagh country. What really happened on that day?'

Long Douglas put his pint pot down on the dust and stared into the flames, shaking his head slowly. 'I didn't kill him either.'

'I know you pinned it on Will. That's why you've chased him so hard. You want him dead so he can't prove you wrong.'

'This is bigger than just me and that cursed Will Jones. Now stop talking and let me rest.'

Within minutes Long Douglas was asleep, and Jim draped a blanket over the top to keep him warm.

Jim had seen sick men come to nefarious life before, so he was careful to set up his swag some distance away, sleeping with his revolver under his arm. He needn't have worried, however, for Long Douglas was on his way to another world, shouting in his sleep at times – repeating a name over and over.

'Curse you Tom Brody,' he yelled. Then, 'Don't shoot him down, Tom.' Finally he cried, 'You can have my share in exchange for my life. You can have it all.'

Towards dawn the calling out stopped, and Jim rose to a golden dawn, awoken by the pure tones of a butcher bird in the trees, and the chattering of fairy wrens that flittered amongst the branches and rocks. Long Douglas was stiff and cold, as dead as any corpse Jim had seen, and he'd come across a few in his days.

Jim closed the dead man's eyelids and used the spade from the packhorse to dig a grave – away from the rocks where the going was easier. He wrapped Long Douglas in a blanket and lowered him down, filled the hole and marked the edges with sticks. It was a lonely duty and he wished Will and Sam were with him.

After a few words over the grave, reflecting on life and death and how enemies too, one day become food for germs and worms, Jim saddled Cartridge. He rode south, wondering who Tom Brody was, and whether he might be the perpetrator of the murder of which Will had been falsely accused.

Chapter Eighteen

An Unexpected Cheque

In a crack between boulders, ten feet from the main shaft of the newly named Blue Dog mine, there lived a blue-tongue lizard, as scaly and tough as the ground itself. About the length of a man's forearm, he was broad and thick with stored fat. His tail was hard to distinguish from his mouth, for both were stumpy and stubby. There was only one difference – his mouth had teeth.

This last fact was something that Little Blue learned early on in his relationship with the blue-tongue, for the young cattle dog hated that reptile like city dogs hate cats. He devoted much of the day to attempting to catch it.

After breakfast, when Will, Sam, Lainey and Johnson had started work, Little Blue would stand a couple of lengths away from the crack, waiting for the fat little lizard to emerge from the cleft in the stone where it lived. Then, every muscle frozen, Blue would watch the creature appear at the opening of his bolthole, tongue flicking from between his lips. The dog was smart enough to wait, even as the lizard moved out into the morning sun.

A foot … two feet … a yard.

Finally now, Little Blue would pounce; and just as quickly the blue-tongue would scurry for the hole. Blue's jaws would close on empty air. It was at this point, bewildered and snuffling at the crack, that the lizard would dart out far enough to give the pup a nip on his sensitive nose.

After a period of confusion, and a canine yelp or two, the game would start all over again. Even after a week, Little Blue was still the sorry loser of this exchange, with a scab on his nose from one particularly deep bite.

**

Meanwhile, the shaft was deepening slowly. The fractured granodiorite of the hillside gave way only with the application of blisters to hands and the power of dynamite. Johnson, it soon proved, was a dab hand with a blasting cap, and when Will asked how a Manning River tit fondler had become so adept at using explosives, he muttered something about blasting old stumps and the like.

The work went well enough, and twelve hours within the allotted time the partners of the Blue Dog Mine loaded their first contractual ten ton of ore onto a company dray, drawn by as fine a team of draught horses as Will had seen. He and Sam took a breather, watching the load heading off towards the Lyver Hills Company battery.

'I won't be expecting much from that lot,' Will said to Sam. 'Never seen so much as a sparkle and we won't, I'm guessing, until we find this darned leader.'

Sam inclined his head in agreement, watching the dray go with his thick arms folded across his chest, and his battered derby hat down low. His hair had grown in the past few weeks, and it hung down past his ears on either side, lank and dusty.

It was only Lainey who held out any hopes for that first load. 'We'll see,' she said. 'Didn't Henry say that there are low values of gold right across the valley?'

'That's true,' said Will. 'He did say that.'

He still didn't hold out much hope.

***

Two days later Henry Sutton rode up to the mine and swung off his horse. From the saddle bags he produced a document, a pencil and what looked like a cheque.

Being hospitable, Will settled the visitor at the fireside and fixed a pint pot of tea in his hands. Johnson and Sam, who had been working on the headgear, came across to listen.

'You men, and ah woman have done well,' said Henry, lighting a cigar. 'Not many small crews get so far so quickly.'

Will took off his hat and wiped his brow with his sleeve. It was a warm day, for August, and he'd been at the face since sparrow's fart. 'Thanks Mr Sutton. We've done our best.'

'Well here's some good news for you – a report on your first crushing,' he said. 'Your ore realised around fourteen pennyweight of gold to the ton – seven ounces nine pennyweight in total. At the current price of three pounds sixpence an ounce, that's not a bad start. Just sign your certificate here, and here's your cheque.'

Will gave a funny little laugh, 'Well that beats everything – I didn't expect a crooked ha'penny from that lot.' He looked at Lainey, who was grinning from ear to ear. It was an exciting moment – a paying lease right from the first week meant that they could buy hardwood for shoring – even pay for extra labour if necessary. It meant that they could eat beef and bread. Most of all it meant that they were not wasting their time and energy.

Will took the processing certificate from Henry Sutton's hand and scanned through it. Then, with a pencil he scrawled his signature on the line, and accepted the cheque with the other hand.

When Sutton had gone, and Will sat down, staring at the cheque, Little Blue left his vigil near the lizard and came to sit at Will's feet, head against his knees.

'So what do we do now?' Lainey asked, while Will scratched his dog's ears.

'Oh I reckon I'll ride to the store at Wilga, cash this barsted cheque an' buy us a bottle or three.' Will said. 'Then tomorrow we get back to work.' He smiled. 'The deeper we go the better this caper is going to pay.'

Chapter Nineteen

Tom Brody

Gamilaroi Jim was not dull enough to ride into the Coonabarabran police station and announce the death of Long Douglas. Yet, he felt a responsibility to the man's widow. Jim was the only one who knew what had happened to the police sergeant, and he had some private possessions in his saddlebags: a few letters that he could not read, a photograph in a tiny frame, and an intricate folding knife.

Jim gave the matter a lot of thought during two weeks spent at the Forked Mountain reserve on the Gunnedah Road. This was a reserve of around five hundred acres where most of his family were living, compressed from their old range that stretched from the mighty Castlereagh River across the plains to the Warrumbungles. This was a time of renewing relationships, remembering old skills, and affirming his place in the world he had been born into; now vastly changed.

A sense of responsibility compelled Jim to ride on, close to Coonabarabran, setting up his camp on the river, fishing and thinking. Later, after a feed of yellowbelly roasted on the coals, he walked into town. It took a few discreet conversations at the Royal Hotel to learn that Long Douglas's residence was on Nandi Street, at the south-eastern end of town.

'Sergeant Douglas ain't been seen for some months,' said the informant. 'Lots a' rumours around – includin' one that he got 'imself shot by Will Jones.'

'That one's not true, bloke,' said Jim. 'I can tell you that for certain.'

Informing a woman of her husband's death seemed like too dour a duty for night-time, so Jim waited until the next morning, broke camp, and rode up George Street with his pack horse trailing behind. Turning up Nand Street, he stopped at the correct address, tied his horses to the front fence and knocked on the door.

A woman in a green house dress appeared at the door, all curves and manicure. Her hair was blonde, with ringlets at the side, yet there was a hardness to her face as she appeared to realise that her caller was not the one she was expecting.

'Can I help you?' she asked.

'Are you Missus Douglas?' Jim asked.

'I am. Who are you and what do you want?'

'You might want to sit down with a cuppa tea, missus. I've brought bad news.'

The woman shrugged, 'Take your boots off if you insist on coming inside.'

Jim did as he was asked, slipping off his 'lastic sided boots, then walking inside and taking a seat at the kitchen table opposite his hostess. After a few barked instructions a maid fetched the kettle from the wood stove, pouring two cups of tea and placing one in front of Jim, the other in front of her mistress.

'Now, I'm very busy, and I don't have time for sitting around with strangers. What is the reason for this intrusion?'

'As I said, it's bad news for you, Missus. Your husband, Sergeant Douglas, is dead. He were thrown from a horse and being alone he got gangrene. I buried him myself.'

Mrs Douglas fingered a chain that hung around her finely sculpted neck. 'Roger is dead? Are you sure it was him?'

'It were surely him.' Jim placed a cloth-wrapped package on the table.

The woman unwrapped it slowly, showing no emotion at the sight of the little knife and her own photograph. She made no effort to open any of the letters. 'Are you sure it wasn't you that killed him? He was on the trail of some dangerous outlaws and you look like one yourself.'

Jim shook his head, 'I wouldn't be sitting here if I had, would I missus?'

'I don't know, would you?'

There was the sound of boots on the stoop and a man entered the house without knocking or removing his footwear. It was the entrance of a man who felt like he belonged here. He was at least six foot tall, with a chin like a shovel blade, and shoulders as wide across and sturdy as a bullock yoke.

'Who the hell are you, and what are you doing here?' growled the man when he saw Jim.

Jim knew the type. This was one of those men who went through life taking whatever he wanted, from whoever they wanted. 'Me name's Jim. And I brung bad news after a long ride. I'm just leavin' now, as it happens,' he said.

'My name is Tom Brody, an' if I see you around here again it'll be the worse for you.'

Jim stared. So this was Tom Brody. The man whose name Long Douglas had called out to so many times in his sleep. He studied the depths behind his eyes and wondered what he knew about the death of John Clarke, and of Joe McCartney, for that matter.

Jim put on his hat and tipped it to the widow, then walked past Tom Brody. Outside, after slipping on his boots he saw that Brody had tethered his horse beside his own, unsaddled it and left a serious work of art sitting on the paling fence.

Tom Brody's saddle was a new Jack Wieneke unit from Roma, high in the back, with practical knee rolls and intricate carvings in the leather flap. It was a saddle that would have cost three months of a working man's salary, and might last ten or more years of hard usage.

Jim's own saddle was almost threadbare, the wooden tree having worn through the leather. It was uncomfortable for both man and horse and he'd been looking for an opportunity to replace it for some time.

From inside he could hear Tom Brody's voice raised, obviously berating Missus Douglas for letting him in. Jim hesitated not a moment longer. He had the girth of his own saddle undone in an instant, and Tom Brody's model off the fence and onto his horse's back to replace it. The contents of the saddlebags – a few cartridges, a folded kerchief and some papers, he dropped to the lawn. Lastly he transferred his own possessions in to replace them. This done, he swung up onto the horse and headed away down the street at a fast trot.

As Jim left town, pointing his horse northwards towards Queensland, he understood at least part of the reason why Long Douglas had cried out the name of Tom Brody in the night, for it seemed to him that Brody had stolen the heart and body of his wife.

Chapter Twenty

Sam smells a rat.

For three more weeks Will, Sam, Lainey and Johnson loaded their ten ton of ore onto a dray bound for the battery, and in due course received a cheque for between seven and eight pounds. Even a one-fourth share was about the same as a stockman's wages, enough to keep them in meat, flour and rum: more than Will had earned on a regular basis for years.

One day Johnson's dog followed him to work and he and Little Blue had their second fight. They were into it in an instant, whirling and biting, holding on and letting go, accompanied by an almost continual series of barks and snarls. Will's dog was not a holder, he was a biter, and his sharp teeth left puncture wounds on the other animal's legs and muzzle.

The other dog, with his terrier ancestry, was bigger and stronger, and he knew how to grip and cancel out the smaller dog's energy. Yet, Little Blue never gave an inch of ground, and his eyes glittered with enjoyment at the contest.

'Rossie, stop that boy,' Johnson yelled half-heartedly, and it was up to Will to enter the fray, wearing gloves, and drag Little Blue out, wet with a little blood and the other dog's saliva.

Separated now, they were tied up in separate areas of the lease, both still glaring and growling, making Will wonder how it was that some dogs got a set against each other right from the start, and others became friends. Just like men, he mused to himself.

***

Sam grew increasingly quiet as the days went by, and one afternoon he started behaving strangely, filling iron pails with samples of stone from various places in the shaft and setting them aside. He wouldn't say a word about what he was up to, but the next morning he told Will that he was not going down the shaft that day.

'Fair enough mate, but what are you gonna do?'

Sam shrugged, but Will watched him when he had a chance. The hardworking Cantonese lugged water up from the tank, then set to crushing rock by placing small amounts in a flour bag and smashing it against a boulder with a sledgehammer.

After an hour or two of crushing rock Sam started panning, still saying nothing, his face serious. Will tried to ignore him, but the strange behaviour was troubling. It made no sense. There was a steam engine and stamp battery available to crush and process the rock—why the hell would Sam want to do it by hand?

It wasn't until that evening, when Sam, Lainey and Will were together, eating a meal of mashed spuds and sausages that Will brought up his friend's strange behaviour.

'You done a bit of panning today,' Will said.

'A bit?' Lainey added. 'He's panned about a hundredweight of rock all crushed to powder.'

Will grinned, 'Our new mate Johnson reckoned you was trying to take the gold out of that rock for yourself.'

Sam looked up. 'No gold here,' he said.

The words troubled Will, but he leaned forward and cleaned his plate into the fire before he commented. 'What do you mean? We got an ounce and a half to the ton last week.'

Sam shook his head. 'No gold here. All that rock I pan today. Not a speck of gold.'

'Maybe you just chose rocks that weren't so good.'

Sam started to look agitated. 'No gold.' He waved an arm back at the lease. 'No gold.'

Will scratched his head, 'Well why does Henry keep payin' us then? Only a crazy person would pay for gold that isn't there.'

Sam shrugged.

'I'll go and see Henry tomorrow,' said Will. 'I'm sure there must be an explanation, or else we've all gone stark ravin' mad.'

Chapter Twenty-one

The London Connection

Ten thousand miles away, across two vast oceans, a small and very energetic man of around forty swung his cane lustily as he walked up Bartholomew Lane towards the London Stock Exchange. With a nod to a few acquaintances, he took the wide path into the complex, greeting the doorman as he passed the piers of granite and marble linings of the new wing, which had, since its construction, been nicknamed 'Gorgonzola Hall.'

Reginald Sutton was a broker with the firm of Grace, Quinn and Donald, and this morning he hastened to a meeting room, where a noisy crew of jobbers, brokers, fund managers and other interested parties had assembled to hear him speak. Reginald walked to the front of the room and placed his right hand on his chest.

'God save the Queen!' he shouted, thereby gaining the attention of everyone present.

'God save the Queen,' they called back, with a few murmured, 'hear hears,' and 'quite rights.'

'Now, my good fellows, I don't intend to waste a minute of your precious time,' Reginald said, delving into his briefcase and removing a stack of booklets, fresh from a print shop in St James Street. 'I have in my hands a prospectus, being for the public share offer of the most exciting venture that will cross your paths this year. The Lyver Hills Mining Company Limited – a new but proven gold mine in Central Queensland, Australia. Rich? Yes. Exciting? Most certainly. You, and your clients have the chance to be part of this exceptional project, and share in very pleasing financial rewards.'

Reginald's eyes shone with excitement. His voice had the rich timbre of a prophet. No one present could doubt that Reginald Sutton believed every word he spoke, and the feeling was contagious. The broker passed around small stacks of the Lyver Hills prospectus, and the room quietened while the pages turned, and experienced financial eyes scanned the projections. There were a few whistles, mentions of ounces to the ton and the exotic names of faraway towns near which the field was located.

'How can we be sure these figures are accurate?' one heavily accented Scots voice said.

Reginald was ready for that. 'Because they have been audited by a Brisbane accounting firm as you can read on the prospectus. Besides, it's not just the Lyver Hills Company pulling out gold like this. There are lots of small miners doing the same – most of them striking payable ore within the first week. You can see their returns there in black and white – and we know because we're processing their ore, making a fat profit for both them and us in the meantime.'

The excitement was contagious – Reginald saw the men starting to nod and talk amongst themselves. He had seen the effect gold, that lovely, lustrous, valuable metal, had on men before, even at a ten-thousand-mile distance from the mines. This meeting was just the beginning – the afternoon newspapers would carry articles and advertisements publicising the venture and inviting share applications from the public. A buzz was required to ensure success, and Reginald was an expert at generating buzz. Who hadn't heard of the Varna Railways float?

Reginald smiled to himself. He knew that after some initial promise, there was very little gold being processed from the Central Queensland field. He didn't care, for by the time anyone had cottoned on to that fact, he and his brother Henry, who was doing the dirty work over in the colony, would be rich. Their fifty per cent share of the company would be worth more than a million pounds, and that would be quietly sold off before the crunch came.

Back in Queensland, Will Jones sat across the desk from Henry Sutton. He explained that when they first arrived Sam had found traces of gold in the gullies, indicating that there was at least some alluvial gold, but that the careful Cantonese man had lately taken samples from all along the shaft and found nothing worth more than a penny. 'There's no gold in that dross we've been cartin' over to ya,' Will said. 'So why are ya payin' us for it?'

A figure appeared at the office door. It was Johnson, wearing a grim face. He walked in without asking and sat down.

'Are you in on this?' asked Will, turning to him furiously.

Johnson said nothing, but made just the slightest movement of his shoulders.

'Damn it,' spat Will. 'What kind of man would spend his days diggin' out worthless rock, knowin' for a fact that it be so?' He moved his attention back to Henry. 'Now tell me the truth, or Lainey, Sam and me will walk away from this place today.'

Henry Sutton made a show of selecting three cigars from the box on his desk, passing them around then striking a vesta. 'I admit,' he started, then paused to get his cigar alight before continuing. 'I admit that you are right, but only partly right.' He passed the still-burning match onto Will, who, never one to refuse good tobacco, used it to good effect on his own cigar. 'There is gold, and this field showed a lot of promise initially. The payable ore though, I must admit, is confined to the three leaders we talked about when you first arrived. The Prodigal, although fabulously rich in a few places that were mined early on, seems to have petered out, while Faith is still returning some gold to our deepest shafts, Hope appears to have been mainly worked to the end of its length.' After Johnson had finished with the still-burning match Sutton took it back, using it to relight his cigar, which had gone out. 'Yet the Lyver Hills Company is about to be floated on the London Stock Exchange, and we need to be able to show that all the leases are producing gold – not just ours.'

'So you're paying us to mine rock so you can make it look like everyone 'ere is on a good thing?'

'That's it exactly,' Henry smiled.

Will pointed through the window at the miners going about their work at the diggings. 'An' all those poor cows out there. Are they all in on this lark? They all know they're bein' paid for cartin' rock?'

'Some know, some don't,' said Henry. 'Some are onto minor pockets of gold, most aren't.'

Will heaved an empty sigh, 'So what do we do?'

'Keep digging, and we'll keep paying.'

'I'm not here to pretend to be a gold miner to earn two pounds a week,' Will sneered. 'You're gonna have to do better 'an that.'

'I can offer you shares in the company.'

Will snorted, 'I don't want shares in a worthless company.' He turned to Johnson. 'Did you know all this?'

Johnson shrugged. 'I guess I did.'

Henry nodded grimly. 'I sent him across with you to keep an eye on things.' He exhaled a stream of cigar smoke that curled and wafted around the rafters. 'It's just five more weeks until the company floats, will you stay 'til then?'

Will crossed his arms. 'Not on the terms we 'ave now. If you want us to keep our traps shut, I want five pound a week each.'

'That is acceptable,' Henry said, 'but just until the float.'

'That's settled then,' said Will. He stood up, opened the lid of Henry's cigar box and took three from the top row, which he transferred into his top pocket. Then he glared at Johnson. 'But we don't want you at the Blue Dog Mine anymore, we'll get our ten tons without your help – and without that damned mongrel of yours.'

Chapter Twenty-two

Rogue Pigeons and Black Cockatoos

When the door had closed behind Will Jones, and he was visible through the window crossing the yard and striding back towards his lease with his chin up and arms swinging, Henry Sutton grinned at Johnson.

'You can let go of the butt of that revolver. Jones is going to play along.'

Johnson took his hand from the pocket of his jacket. 'Will Jones is a rogue pigeon – and I've said it right from the start. He won't fly with the flock.'

'I agree with you. That's why I sent you over to work on the lease with him.'

'Seems like I'm not wanted there any more in any case – and that's fine by me. But who's gonna keep an eye on him now?'

Sutton shrugged, 'Five pounds a week will keep him quiet until after the float.'

'I'm not so sure.'

'Trust me. Will Jones will take the money and shut his mouth.'

'And if he doesn't?'

Sutton stabbed the butt of his cigar into the cut-glass ash tray, 'In that case, there are plenty of old mine shafts around, that a careless larrikin like Will Jones might fall into.'

***

When Will returned from the meeting, Sam and Lainey were sitting in their places near the fire, with quart pots of tea and slices of oatmeal and honey cake, still hot from the camp oven. Will took a seat, shared the cigars around and passed on everything that Henry Sutton had told him, talking between mouthfuls of cake and gulps of tea.

'We're to be paid five pounds a week for five weeks, until this company thing floats on some stock exchange, whatever the devil that means.' He looked at Sam. 'I guess you'd know what it's all about.'

'I know enough,' said Sam. 'They tryin' to make a lot of money out of nothing. Rich men makin' more money from poor fellows like us.'

'Five weeks,' Lainey repeated. 'Jim should be back by then an' we can ride off together. Where's Johnson?'

There was a loud arrrk, arrrk from above, and they all looked skyward as four or five red-tailed black cockatoos flew over from west to east. The magnificent birds had always seemed like good luck to Will, but now he wasn't so sure.

'Johnson ain't comin' back,' said Will when the birds had receded over the hills. 'I told 'im not to show 'is face here again – I'll bet a penny to a pound that 'e was only 'ere to spy on us fer Sutton. Oh he knew how to work, I'll give 'im that, but 'e was prob'ly tellin' Sutton every word we said.'

'Ah bugger that,' spat Lainey. 'Spies and all. Come on Will, what d'ya reckon? Can't we just ride off.'

Will shook his head. 'Five weeks of digging a wee bit of rock for five pound a week is more than we'll get for honest yakka anywhere else. Let's keep on until the cheques stop, then if Jim's back all well an' good. We'll go find somethin' better.'

Lainey clamped her lips together and gave an emphatic nod. 'Well I say we should live it up while we're here. There's still that shanty down at Wilga. We can get ten ton a week out of this barsted shaft without hardly trying, an' have a good time while we're at it.'

Will grinned back at her. 'You ain't had a flash a' brilliance in five years, Lainey, but that's a fine thought.'

Sam heaved a sigh and came to his feet. 'Drink, work, yeah orright, but I wish Jim was back here. Things ain't the same without that fellow.'

Will looked down at the smouldering fire. Sam was right. They needed Jim back.

Chapter Twenty-three

Showdown East of the Pillaga

After four hours of hard riding from Coonabarabran, Jim spotted a good flat camp in a clearing that had been used by travellers before. It was a picturesque site, surrounded by cypress, ironbark and Pilliga box. A spring-fed pool, with lilies scattered over the surface was the real attraction.

To the accompaniment of frogs and crickets, Jim unsaddled his pack and riding horses, then laid his new acquisition – that special Jack Wieneke saddle – on a handy part of a fallen branch, then made his camp as normal.

He cooked a feed of fresh bloody beef liver that he had bought from the butchery in town, then took his hatchet out, ground the blade to a fresh edge on his whetstone, and took a wander around the nearby trees. He selected a branch from a bull-oak tree, chopped it out and took it back to camp. He used his knife to whittle away branchlets and to shave off the bark.

When this was done, he unrolled his swag, stuffed items from his gear inside to make it look like he was sleeping there, and built up the fire. In pride of place, in plain view, he sat Tom Brody's saddle so that it would be visible in the firelight. Now he took his rifle and the club he had made, a few hundred yards back down the track where he hid behind a thick trunk.

Not thirty minutes passed before Jim heard a rider mooching along cautiously up the track. Even with the meanness of the moon Jim could see that it was Tom Brody, and he heard the man's hiss of indrawn breath – seeing his own saddle displayed so invitingly in the firelight. Jim watched Brody dismount and tether his horse, take a Colt revolver from a holster and check the load. While he was thus occupied, Jim left his hiding place, and, moving like a ghost in the night, padded silently up behind the man he now regarded as an enemy.

With a silent rush he clocked the big man on the back of the head with the club. Bull-oak was one of the hardest timbers known. Tom Brody fell like a widow-maker branch from a gum tree to the ground. Jim bent to one knee and checked both eyes in turn.

It took him ten minutes to drag the unconscious man up to camp and truss his wrists and ankles. This done, and with Brody's horse grazing nearby with his own plant, Jim made a billy of tea and filled a pint pot. His carbine lay across his lap, and he passed the time pushing cartridges into the loading port, then levering them out again, one by one.

He was still drinking tea and playing with the rifle when Tom Brody came back to consciousness. It was almost comical to watch. His eyes flicked open; stared across the camp at Jim. He moaned and tried to move one hand to massage his head. Realised he couldn't. Glared at Jim again. Then came a roar like a bull in rut.

'You!' Tom Brody shouted. He fought the ropes like a tiger, before finally exhausting himself. This was followed by some of the most inventive and colourful swearing Jim had heard, including allusions to Jim's birth, his character, and the friends he chose to ride with.

By the time Jim had finished his tea, Tom Brody had run out of bile to fuel his tirade, and he was sitting, breathing with his mouth open, glaring at his captor.

'Evenin' bloke,' Jim said, tipping one hand to his head in a mock salute.

'I'll cut your black throat for this,' Brody warned with menace.

'You won't get the chance,' said Jim. 'I could 'a' cut your white throat, if I'd wanted to.'

'I want my saddle back.'

'I like it,' said Jim, 'so I'm keepin' it. Besides, it were a handy way of gettin' you to follow me.'

'You're a fool. No man on God's earth wants the likes of me on his tail.'

'There's a reason, Mr Tom Brody. You an' me have business to discuss. One of me best mates – Will Jones – stands accused of a murder that Long Douglas tried to pin on 'im. I was there for that cruel man's last hours and he cried out certain things. It seems to me that you might know information that would see me mate pardoned.'

Tom Brody sneered, 'Will Jones is a low-life fool. I'm betting he's done murder before today.'

'Speakin' of low-lifes,' said Jim, 'how long've you been beddin' Long Douglas's missus for? Hell, you didn't even know he was dead and it seems to me that you've been livin' in her house.'

'That's none of your damn business.' Brody hawked in the back of his throat and spat. The result fell short, landing in the fire and sizzling.

Jim ignored it, 'I'll let you go, with your horse, if you tell me who shot John Clarke, and why he was carrying a package of poison that killed McCartney out at Kyungra Station.'

'You'll let me go? Do you think I'd take a black fellow's word on that?'

Jim shrugged. 'That's up to you, bloke, but otherwise I might just harness up that horse of yours an' use him to snig ya deep into the forest an' leave you there. No one would find you – not until you started to smell anyhow.'

Tom Brody laughed, as if at a very funny joke. 'Alright then, I shot John Clarke. So what? Try getting me to say that in front of a judge.'

'Why did ya shoot him, bloke?'

'Well the poison idea was hatched by Long Douglas's himself. The three of us, Me, Joe McCartney and Long Douglas had been shareholders in that Kyungra Station for a lot of years. Long Douglas wanted to sell out – he had gambling debts you see, but McCartney wouldn't hear of it, and neither could he raise the funds to buy us other partners out. Long Douglas's creditors were pressing on him, so he hatched a plan to kill off McCartney at arm's length, with Clarkie ridin' north to Queensland to find someone to carry the package.

'I wasn't a fan of the scheme myself, and I rode to where Clarkie was setting off, and the three of us argued. I lost me temper and shot Clarkie to stop him from going. I didn't mean to kill the poor bastard – even worse he'd already got on his horse and it bolted with him dying in the saddle. That's when you an' Will Jones just had to be in the wrong place at the wrong time.'

Jim took it all in, 'One little fact don't make sense, bloke. The package with the poison was signed LHD. Long Douglas's first name was Roger.'

'A bit of a joke. We used to call him Long Harry – LHD." It was something that Joe McCartney would know, but not anyone else who might come across the package. Now let me go. You said you would. And I want my saddle too.'

Jim shook his head, 'I told ya. That saddle is mine now. In return for having to go on the run for a murder that you done yourself.' He stood, stretched, then fetched Brody's horse. Then, with the reins looped around his elbow he cut the bonds on his captive's ankles, helping him to mount up. He returned the Colt revolver, after opening the cylinder and throwing the cartridges into the scrub. Last of all he untied Tom Brody's wrists.

Brody looked as if he was about to ride off when he reached somewhere into his clothing, or perhaps the saddle bag, and withdrew a tiny derringer pistol, aiming it as fast as a snake at Jim. He fired before Jim could raise his carbine.

The ball struck Jim deep, then there was a clatter of hooves as Tom Brody's horse skittered away.

Jim finally managed to raise the carbine and fire one despairing shot, and by then he was falling to the roadway.

Chapter Twenty-four

The Man in the Mist

Will ordered a final glass of rum at the little shanty at Wilga, three miles from the Blue Dog Mine, and took a sip. It no longer had the bite it had earlier on in the evening but still he enjoyed the warmth in his gut and mind. It was late, the moon three days past full but already shining through the treetops, and Will guessed that it must be around midnight.

Little Blue, quiet under the table, gave a whimper and looked hopefully up at his master. Sam had left the shanty more than an hour ago, and Lainey had stayed at camp tonight. Little Blue was ready to head home.

Yet, something was troubling Will – more than just a cool breeze through the stony hills. Ever since he arrived he had felt that someone was watching him from outside the lantern-lit shanty.

Twice he had left his bench to walk around in the shadows, but there were men, and a few women with them, camped all through the area, their fires twinkling between lancewood and wattle trunks. He saw nothing out of the ordinary, but still he remained on edge.

With a calming hand he reached down and stroked Little Blue's ears. 'We're headin' home in a minute,' he said. 'Just making sure there's nothin' out there that's gonna bother us, fair enough?'

Little Blue cocked his head at an angle, as if working hard to understand what his master was saying. Finally, satisfied, he settled down again. Will turned his attention back to his rum, thinking, not for the first time that perhaps his little crew should pack up and leave the area. It seemed unlikely that any real good was going to come of staying longer, even with five pounds a week each coming in.

Oh, they were still working the shaft hard enough, with Sam still optimistic about their prospects. In any case, coming up with ten ton of material a week was easy enough, and if they hadn't extracted enough from the shaft itself, they simply shovelled in old spoil that was laying around in piles.

Will always had the knack of knowing when one more drink would be too many, and he decided that no good would come of staying here longer tonight. Drinking down his last mouthful, Will pocketed his pipe and tobacco pouch, stood and put on his hat. With a nod to the owner he turned and walked out from under the shadow of the bough roof, towards his horse, tied to a rail with the saddle behind him.

Throwing on the leather and tightening the girth took no time at all, and soon Will, with Little Blue padding along beside him, was riding back towards home. He was in no rush, despite the late hour, and he maintained a walking gait through the scrub, and a trot in open country.

The cool night had raised a light ground mist, and this gave the night a ghostly quality. This was enough to disturb a man's mood on its own, but worse was to come. Up ahead, on the track, he saw the figure of a man, standing tall and proud. Little Blue started to growl.

Will was not easily spooked, and he rode on towards the figure, but he made sure that his revolver was within reach, taking the reins with one hand so his other was free.

'Will Jones,' the man called.

Will felt a shiver of supernatural dread, and the horse, catching the mood, stopped, unwilling to go on. Forced to dismount in order to continue, Will used a hand on the bridle to encourage his mount onward.

As Will drew closer, the moment of recognition came. 'Luke Phillips?' he cried. 'Is that you?'

'Oh yes, it's me alright. I should slap your face for what you done to me – leavin' me hog-tied on the side of the track and ridin' away like that. I could have died.'

'Maybe so,' mused Will as memories of the incident a few months earlier came back to him. 'But I still wouldn't try slappin' me on the face.'

Phillips wasn't finished his tirade; 'You left me tied up on the side of a track, and carried Lainey, the love of my life, a thousand mile away. It's taken me all these months to find you. Where is she? Take me to her.'

Will shook his head sadly. It seemed that Lainey's husband – for this was him – Luke Phillips, didn't know when to give up. He was the last person he'd expected to find stalking them. He coughed, a little embarrassed for the other man, then said, 'Might be a wasted journey, for Lainey's told me plenty of times that she'd rather stick her tongue in an ant-nest than go home with you.' Little Blue punctuated this statement by sitting back and growling.

Phillips crossed his arms in front of his chest. 'She's my wife, by golly, and I want to see her.'

'I'll take you to her. What happens then is up to Lainey herself.'

'I'll get me horses,' said Luke, and he was soon tagging along behind, with two pack horses in train.

When finally they reached the mine Will helped the visitor to unload his packs and see to the animals. This done he went to the fireplace, threw on some sticks from the pile and set the billy on to boil. He threw in some tea leaves and made a brew for each of them by the warming blaze.

'See that tent over there,' said Will, pointing a finger at a grubby sheet of canvas thrown over poles. 'That's Lainey's tent.'

They drank down their tea. Luke was obviously having an attack of nerves now that he had come so close. He'd taken off his hat and was running one hand through his lank dark hair, as if trying to comb it into some kind of order. 'Maybe it'd be best not to wake 'er up now,' he muttered into his pint pot. 'If I wait 'til morning she might be more welcoming.'

'Up to you mate,' said Will. 'But from my experience Lainey aren't any more good-natured first thing in the morning than a black snake. If I was you I'd get it over with.'

This conversation became irrelevant, for the sound of fingers scratching on canvas came, and Lainey herself appeared at the door of her tent, dressed in her usual bed-time garb of pantaloons and an oversized man's shirt.

'I knew it!' she cried. 'That voice couldn't be any other than me 'usband. Luke Phillips! What in the name of tarnation are you doin' here?'

And didn't Will smile when Lainey's husband came over all bashful and shy!

'Well I wasn't gonna trouble you tonight. I'll sleep in me swag tonight and we can talk in the morning.'

'The hell you will, you think I'd let me own 'usband sleep outside with the dingoes? Get over 'ere now.'

Luke looked at Will, shrugged, then hurried over to the tent, stopping only at the entrance to remove his boots when Lainey demanded that he do so.

Will watched him go. He heard the buttons of the tent close up again, followed by the sound of laughter and soft talking in the night. He looked up at the stars and wished he didn't have to be alone tonight either. Even later, as he lay in his swag, the girl in the postcard, the love of his life, failed to give him comfort.

Chapter Twenty-five

Wounded

Jim lay on the surface of the track, still surprised and angry at himself for what had just happened. Delving down along his belly he found the stinging hole in the skin of his gut. It was small, more like a tear than a hole, and the sound of the shot had indicated a small calibre, maybe even a .22. Moving his now bloody hand around to his back, he found no exit wound. That made sense, for the worst of the pain was deep inside.

Jim raised his head off the gravel, seeing in the light of the rising moon that the other man had reined in at a hundred yards, and turned back to face him—most likely in the process of reloading his Colt. Jim knew that Brodie still wanted that saddle, and now, besides, he would seek revenge on Jim for trussing him up and keeping him captive. Jim's carbine would make Brodie wary, but he might simply wait to see if Jim would die or pass out.

Jim reached down for the Henry repeater, settled into the prone shooting position, and fitted the stock into his shoulder. The post and vee iron sights were hard to see in the night, and it was strange – the hands that could always be relied on to be rock-steady were shaking like those of a man coming off the drink.

In any case, Jim rejected the idea of taking a shot at Brodie now. Apart from the practical issue of hitting his mark, gunning a man down from a distance was murder and he did not want another troop of police on his tail.

Jim looked at the eastern horizon, where the moon was clear of the horizon, and flirting with the trees. Once it passed the canopy it would be as good as daylight. If there were any tricks to be played it had to be now. Brodie, he suspected, had no intention of riding away without finishing Jim off and taking the saddle.

Jim waited for a darker moment when the rising moon was deep behind the thickest scrub, and then he slithered across the track into the bushes near his camp. The more he moved the more he bled, and once or twice he had to stop, doubled over to bring the pain under control. He snatched a look back up the track, and Brodie still didn't seem to have moved.

Keeping to the scrub, Jim hunted up Cartridge, and found the branch where he had hung the stallion's tack, fitting bit, bridle and reins while he held his rifle under his arm.

There was also a fully-laden pack and a good horse that would have to be left behind, but Jim raided those supplies and filled his pockets with tobacco, matches, some flour and tea.

Jim looked down the roadway and saw that Tom Brodie was walking his horse in closer now, for the moon was clear and he would soon be able to see that Jim had moved. The young Gamilaroi man could have ridden off bareback, but he wanted that Jack Wieneke saddle, and to get it he needed to go into the firelight. He wanted the saddle in exchange for the trouble Tom Brodie had caused to him and his mates, by shooting a man and pinning it on Will Jones. It was just one small thing that helped even the score.

The most important thing, Jim decided, was to show Tom Brodie that he was still armed and dangerous. He raised the rifle, leaned against the side of a trunk, and aimed a yard or two above the other man's head. The report was loud, numbing to the ears, and in Jim's experience this was louder for a man in front of the firearm.

Tom Brodie's horse reared, and then, as the rider gained control, they turned and galloped back down the road. Jim didn't wait to see how far Tom Brodie went. He staggered into the clearing, leading the horse. He grabbed the saddle, threw it on and buckled the girth. Still holding the Henry carbine, he had one foot in the stirrup when a spasm of pain stopped him cold and he had to lean over, close his eyes, and wait until it eased.

Now he tried again, and he heard a shout from down the track, just as he settled into the saddle leather. Responding to urgent pressure from Jim's heels, the stallion sprung into a gallop; getting away down the northwards track in an instant, with Brodie coming hard behind him.

Wounded or not, Jim gave himself a chance – few men could ride like him, and Tom Brodie was heavy – he probably weighed twice as much. No whip on earth can incite a good overloaded horse to beat a good lightly laden one. Jim felt confident that as long as he could stop the wound in his gut from bleeding away his strength he had a chance.

Chapter Twenty-six

Fool's Gold

It was a strange thing, but Lainey didn't throw her husband out the next morning, nor even the one after that. By the third day Luke Phillips seemed to be a fixture at the camp. No one said much about it, but Lainey changed her habits noticeably, taking trouble with her hair and washing a little more often.

'What's that blue thing in yer hair?' Will asked her one evening as his sister returned from the screened washtub at a far corner of the lease.

Lainey turned on him furiously, 'It's a ribbon, ya dullard. Ain't it normal fer a woman to make 'erself presentable?'

Will retorted, 'It might be normal fer a woman, but it ain't normal for you.' He couldn't figure out why she was taking so much trouble for a man she'd run out on.

Luke, as Will knew, was a hard worker from way back, and laying about the camp was not his style. When fetching firewood didn't fill in the time Luke made some improvements around the camp. He wasn't a bad bush carpenter, after all. Next he grabbed a pickaxe and insisted on taking his turn down the mine shaft.

'There aren't no gold here,' Will confided in him. 'At least nothing to speak of.'

'What? Why in blazes are you diggin' then?' asked Luke, holding the pickaxe by the handle and leaning on it.

'Well,' said Will. 'A couple of English brothers own the big mining company yonder, and its gonna float on some stock exchangin' outfit or other. They are payin' us good money to dig up ten ton of rock each week, so they can chuck in a few specks of the good stuff here and there, and make it look like the whole field here is as rich as King Solomon's own mines.'

'What a lurk!' exclaimed Luke. 'I imagine they'll make a fortune out of it too. So there's no gold here at all?'

'Fool's gold,' laughed Lainey.

Sam had just walked up, took his seat and removed his hat. 'A little gold. Three gold leaders here – used to be.'

'Faith, Hope and the Prodigal,' continued Lainey. 'An' we reckoned on puttin' our mine right here to chase the Prodigal – supposed to be the richest one of the lot, in places. But the parts a'those leaders that were found, down the valley there, were worked out, an' they ain't reappeared.'

'They should have called them Misery, Heartbreak and Bullshit,' said Will. 'If it wasn't for Henry Sutton's cash money we would have moved on weeks ago.'

Luke shrugged, 'Well you've still got to fill the dray with ten ton of rock each week, so it won't hurt me to help do that.' He looked at Lainey. 'I'm hoping when this is all over that my wife will ride back south with me … home.'

Lainey shook her head and spat on the ground. 'You men don't know when you're well off. Right here you got a wife, a home,' she pointed a finger at the grubby tent they were sharing, 'an' gainful employment, and now you want to drag me back to that damned farm of yours.'

'Is it too much to ask,' said Luke, 'for a man to want his wife to be beside him on the land?'

'Too much to ask fer me,' said Lainey emphatically. 'Now take that pick and get to work, or I won't be sharin' a swag with you neither.'

Luke hefted his pick and waved it at Will. 'Show me where to go and what to do and I'll get busy at it.'

Will led his sister's husband to the shaft and down the ladder. At the bottom, slush lantern in hand, he walked along the drift to the face. 'That's where we're digging. Don't go faster than we can shore it up, and if you see any cracks get out of there as quick as you can.'

'What if I see some gold?' asked Luke.

'You won't – like Lainey said, it'll be fool's gold if you do.'

***

Funnily enough, Little Blue, who didn't take to strangers, as a rule, accepted Lainey's husband after a day or two. He liked Luke's boots most of all, and rare was the morning that didn't start with that poor man bellowing darkly, 'What's that fandangled pup done with me boot this time?'

'Just find it an' stop blamin' Little Blue,' Lainey would say.

This was followed by the tromping of feet, and an eventual, 'Here it is. Now don't take it again, will you Blue?'

And for almost a week this routine went on. There was only room for one miner at the face, and the four of them took turns, with another barrowing the rock along the drift, another operating the windlass, and the other snatching a rest or cooking.

One late afternoon the crew came up from the shaft, and took their places around the campfire. Lainey had ridden to Wilga for supplies, and brought back bottled beer. She'd just filled four mugs when Luke took a long swig and made an observation.

'That was a long hour, that last shift at the face,' he said. 'But I did see some of that fool's gold you were talking about. By calamity I never knew it was such pretty stuff. A whole fandangled seam of it.' He brightened and turned to Will. 'It's lucky you warned me not to fall for it.'

It was a strange thing, but Will was no longer there. Beers forgotten, Sam and Will were running for the top of the shaft, with Lainey not far behind. Not one to miss out on what seemed like fun, Luke joined them, with Little Blue barking from the top as the ladder creaked and groaned with their combined weight.

The four of them crowded along the drift, all the way to the face, packed so close they could scarcely breathe. Will, who'd had the presence of mind to bring a lantern, lifted it high. None of them said a word at first, though Lainey swore something unintelligible under her breath.

Will felt a lump in his throat. This wasn't fool's gold, it was rich, native reef gold, yellow, almost orange in places, impregnated and surrounded by the quartz seam, and as thick as a man's leg.

'The Prodigal,' breathed Sam. 'We found it.'

'Oh God yes, we found it,' said Will.

'So this ain't fool's gold then?' asked Luke.

Will shook his head. 'No. It's a seam of gold worth more than ya farm, you flukey barsted.'

'Holy Hell,' said Lainey aloud. 'I can't bloody believe it.'

Despite the lack of space Will managed to shake hands with Sam first, then the others in turn. Then he said, 'When we go up top, no one is to whoop, no one is to holler, or say one thing out of the ordinary. No one up there must know about this, least of all bloody Johnson or Henry Sutton.'

The silence stretched on for a long time. They were all busy with their own thoughts of how the gold would affect them. Finally, when they filed slowly back up top, they picked up their beers and drank to good health and long life, just as they had on other occasions.

Still, Will couldn't ever remember seeing a smile on Sam's face like the one he wore now, and Lainey's eyes sparkled like the brightest stars in the sky. They'd had some fun together, but never a windfall like this.

How would they get the gold out and make fair value from it? That was the question.

Chapter Twenty-seven

Wild Dog

When that Warrumbungle country filled with the yellow glow of dawn, refracting from the cliff faces, and glowing iridescent on the trees, a wedge-tailed eagle flew from his perch on Bluff Mountain. Flying north over the Pilliga he spotted a horseman, one of the people he had known from his time as a fledgling; a man from the old clans of the plains.

It was obvious, even from a height, that the rider was wounded, for he held a hand to his gut, and sometimes gave a cry of pain when his horse stumbled hard or the ground grew rough. He rode fast, even so, and the reason for that was obvious. Some miles back, a big white man rode hard in pursuit.

Interested in the contest, the eagle shadowed the pair as they hurried north towards the Namoi River. Conditions for flying were perfect, with strong thermals as the day wore on, and the eagle remained aloft without effort.

Wounded or not, though, that Gamilaroi fella was clever and brave. He swum his horse across the big river near the junction with Spring Creek, but the man who chased him baulked at the deep water. Instead he rode around through the town of Narrabri to the road bridge, then went back to find the trail, which had been cleaned and anti-tracked by then, with clever hands and bushcraft.

When the white man finally gave up — turned around and took the road south again to Coonabarabran, the eagle flew high above, and watched him until the night drew close and it was time to return to his perch.

***

Old dingo was sniffing 'round his country north of the Namoi later that night when he caught the scent of fresh blood, and followed it along to the banks of a waterhole, where red clay banks were lighted by the flames of a small fire.

There, on the banks the dingo saw a brown man, hunched over, tears of pain running down his cheeks in bitter furrows. His fingers were red from delving into a wound in his gut. At length the man looked up, and saw the dingo. He did not seem shocked, but his horse, tethered to an overhanging tree just behind him, nickered nervously.

'Hullo there, warrigal dog,' said the man. 'Don't look at me like I'm a lump of tucker old bloke. I'm a long way from that yet.'

The dingo stopped, maybe fifteen paces away. When the man made no hostile move, the animal settled onto his haunches.

'I was careless ya know,' said the man. 'This bugger called Tom Brody put a bullet in me with a sneaky little derringer he had hidden. Now I gotta get that slug out so things can heal up inside – 'an this hole's still not big enough for me fingers. I reckon that if I can widen the hole I'll likely be able to grasp it. Them derringers are easy to hide but they don't pack much punch.'

The dingo watched as the brown man took a little knife from a sheath and gripped it carefully, leaning down to place the point into the hole in his gut—the source of the blood—then crying out in agony as he cut sideways, letting the knife fall beside him as he gathered himself for an even greater effort—forcing his fingers inside, the blood smell saturating the air now.

Finally, the brown man went into some kind of paroxysm, shaking like a dying bird. This time it took a while for him to recover. At length, however, the shaking stopped, and he held up a bloody thumb and forefinger, something small gripped between them. 'Just a little bit of lead,' said the man. 'But one of these will kill you dead, old warrigal. You watch out for men with guns, and the bullets that fly from them. You keep clear of them orright?'

The brown man seemed to be in no hurry to stand, but rowed himself on his bottom to the water where he washed the wound, though a fresh flow kept coming. When this was done he dug a hole on the bank and extracted a handful of clay. This he used to plug the wound, forcing it deep inside.

'This clay very special,' Jim told the dingo. 'My people been using it for a long time. Stops that bleeding right up, and it's got strong medicine in it besides.'

Finally, with an effort that showed on his face, and the muscles on his bare chest and stomach standing proud, the man stood up: moving away to where his horse was tethered, and the dingo watched as he mounted up.

'I've got mates to catch up with. Long, long way, so I can't stop. See you later old fella,' said the man.

And he rode off into the night.

Chapter Twenty-eight

The Golden Garden

Will couldn't help feeling protective about the richness of their find, so he took to closing the shaft at night with sheets of tin. He also moved his swag closer to the mine headgear. With Little Blue keeping watch beside him, no prowler would approach the mine at night without rousing the camp.

Even so, Will was finding it hard to sleep. He was sick with worry. If he declared the find to Henry Sutton he imagined that trouble would follow. Yet, getting the gold out and selling it under the noses of other diggers would be no picnic either.

As happened so often, it was Sam who provided the solution. He leased a plot of land on the arable flats near a waterhole on Black Wattle Creek, three miles away from the claim. He started by building a brush fence around two acres near the river, then tilled the earth with borrowed tools. When the plot was ready he planted tomatoes, melons, cucumbers and more.

'No gold aroun' here,' Sam would tell anyone who'd listen. 'Best make money from garden.'

Within a couple of weeks Sam had not only planted his first crop, but had also dug an underground storehouse in the midst of his seedling beds – six feet straight down into the earth, supported by hardwood slabs he split from along the creek, with a cavernous space inside. The top was itself a thick slab of coolabah, hidden some eighteen inches under the earth, with loose soil on top so no one would suspect that it was there.

It was up to Luke, Will and Lainey to extract the rich ore from the Prodigal leader, and each morning, when Sam rode off to work his garden he carried in his saddlebags anything up to a couple of pounds of gold-rich ore. Then, in the safety of the overhanging trees by the creek he would crush the ore, pick out the pure lumps, then pan the rest to extract almost pure gold.

It was back-breaking work, but Sam didn't mind. He recognised the face of good fortune when it smiled upon him. When the work was done he cached the treasure in that carefully prepared hiding place. Through it all, the partners delivered their weekly ten tons of dross to the company battery and received their commission each week with good grace.

These happenings, however, did not go unnoticed. It was Johnson who saw the change in demeanour of the men and woman who worked the Blue Dog Mine, and he took to hanging round a little, wandering past with his dog, a habit that led to a third vicious fight between Will's blue heeler and that mongrel terrier Rossie.

One early morning Johnson trailed Sam all the way to the beginnings of his market garden, and wasted a morning watching the Cantonese man transplant seedlings and spread manure. Still. Johnson's suspicions were fully aroused.

One night, in the mine office, with a lantern burning yellow, and three men playing poker for crowns and guineas, Johnson made his feelings known.

'They're up to something,' he said to Henry Sutton. 'That Will Jones and his mates. Whatever it is it ain't good news for us.'

Sutton held his cards steady and glared at Johnson. 'The float's only a matter of days away. We can't afford problems. Find out what's going on, there's a good fellow.'

***

It was a funny thing, but in the evenings, Will Jones had got in the habit of climbing the tallest of the nearby hills, just to the west of their lease. The walk allowed him to stretch his legs and exercise Little Blue, who bounded along, sniffing out wallabies in the crackling dry grass, rolling in the dust and generally carrying on like young dogs do.

'Get back 'ere ya little barsted,' Will called now and then, but there was a gentle humour in his voice, for he loved to see the young dog run free.

Little Blue was full grown now, at least in height, with a thick coat of icy white-blue. He still had his bandit-masks over both eyes, and it gave him a rascally look. Yet, he had also developed the best qualities of his breed – a good brain, patience and loyalty.

At the top of the hill, Will sat down on one of the many granodiorite boulders, with the dog beside him. There, with a view in all directions he smoked his pipe and fondled the dog's ears while the sunset glowed vermillion over the wild country around.

Will had lost weight, in those last few months, and his arms, flanks and back were lean and tight with muscle. The finding of the gold had brought a sense of responsibility, and this was visible in his eyes, along with the glitter of dreams of a future that might be a little easier to fund than it had been in the past.

Lost in thought, Will noticed that Little Blue had pricked up his ears and was looking into the scrub to the south-west. Will followed the direction of his gaze. In the failing light he could see a horseman riding fast towards the diggings.

Will stood up, then jumped lightly up onto the boulder he had been sitting on. From that vantage point he peered into the distance. Could it be? he whispered to himself.

As the rider neared Will noted the dark skin of his bare chest. It was Jim; it had to be, with no pack horse and a lean and flat mount that looked like it had been ridden hard and long.

Will waved his hat and gave a cooee, loud and clear, pitched over the evening squabble of lorikeets in the branches above. Pretty soon he saw Jim veer towards him.

Jim looked like he had been to hell and back. There was a new scar on his flank and his face seemed pasty and ill. Even so, there was a wild building warmth in Will's chest at seeing Jim again. Mates are like brothers, and they are made to ride together, not apart. Jim had been gone for too long.

When Jim came up, he all but tumbled from his horse, and Will had to put his arms out and stop him from falling. He saw in his friend's eyes the extremes of the journey home, and the obvious rawness of the wound still fresh in his abdomen. Little Blue could see it too, for he reached up with his forelegs against Jim's thighs, whining plaintively.

Will wanted to say a lot of things, but instead he simply said; 'You took your bloody time.' When Jim didn't answer, he helped his mate back up onto the saddle. 'Let's take you down to camp, Jim mate. And get a feed into you.'

Chapter Twenty-nine

The Float

In Gorgonzola Hall, in London Town, Reginald Sutton watched the chalkboards in that maniacal room, where jobbers scrambled, brokers shouted to be heard above the din, and the faces of men showed despair or triumph depending on the profits of the day. It was a strange leveller, the stock exchange, where Rothschilds rubbed shoulders with Whitechapel scrappers who had worked themselves out of the gutter and stayed out only by the progress of trade from day to day.

'Lyver Hills Mining Company, the latest thing from the colony of Queensland,' shouted a jobber in a high voice that rose above the chaos. 'Eight shillin's a share, for a total market capitalisation of two million pounds.'

Reginald was feeling pleased with the progress of the float so far. Subscriptions had opened some nine days earlier, and the offices of Grace, Quinn and Donald at Cheapside had been busy with a tide of mail-in requests and small investors arriving in person. Mining companies were hot property on the London Stock Exchange, and the Australian colonies were seen as 'safe' options compared to the likes of Argentina or Mexico.

Shouts of 'Buy ten thousand at four-fifths,' and 'three thousand at par,' filled the room, and Reginald watched as the remaining, unsubscribed shares sold off, and the real trade began — some early buyers taking a profit by releasing some shares back on to the market.

This started to drive up the price — ten shillings, then fourteen. By dinner time the shares were nudging eighteen shillings and now came the time in which Reginald had to use every ounce of his experience and instinct.

He walked up to a broker he used, not from his own firm, and whispered in his ear. In so doing he released a block of one hundred thousand shares that were registered in his own name. These were snapped up, with no shortage of buyers calling for ten or even twenty thousand.

And through that afternoon's trade, Lyver Hills Mining Company shares were the most sought-after issue at the exchange, with buy orders going unfulfilled and the price rising so steadily that Reginald took a gamble and waited until nearly four pm to start releasing the rest of the shares held in his own name and that of his brother Henry.

The influx told on the price, and by the time the market closed the price had dropped back down to fifteen shillings. It didn't matter. Brothers Reginald and Henry Sutton had made a profit of more than a hundred thousand pounds each, all for the relatively modest investment of around ten thousand, and two years of work.

A hundred thousand pounds was enough for a man to live a life of relative luxury without an iota of work, for the rest of his life. It was enough to buy twenty or thirty houses and live off the rent. More exciting still, it was enough to provide serious investment clout, and to offer opportunities to make more money still.

Reginald could scarcely contain himself on the way to the telegraph office, whistling and swinging his umbrella lustily. Then, breezily fronting the clerk, he took the proffered pad of paper. He wrote:

DEAR BROTHER SUCCESS IS OURS STOP ALL SHARES SOLD CONGRATULATIONS TO US BOTH STOP RICH REWARDS FOR HARD WORK AND PLANNING ENDS

The telegram paid for, and flashing its way across the world to Clermont, Queensland, Reginald hailed a hansom cab and sat up behind the driver.

'Where to, fine sir?' asked the driver.

'Wiltons in Saint James,' replied Reginald. It was one of London's oldest and most expensive restaurants. He'd had the foresight, and confidence, to book a table for he and some of his best friends, for the celebration he'd hoped to have. One of those friends, a senior clerk at Barings, had a daughter, just turned nineteen, who would be a fine adornment if he could only turn her head. Being a very rich man, still with relative youth, was a good start.

***

Far away, in Queensland, on the very diggings that had just been the subject of that frenzy on the Stock Exchange, Jim was responding to rest and good food, regaining his good humour and vitality.

Will calculated that Jim had ridden more than a thousand miles in thirteen days, eating only bush tucker on the way. He was permitted no work, in those early days, and Will and the others listened breathlessly to his stories of Tom Brody, the death of Long Douglas, and the shooting that made his return so painful.

Within a week, however, the scar on Jim's gut had fully closed, and he had gained a little weight. His attitude to mining work had not changed, and he would not set foot underground, but he was happy to assist Sam with the garden, and cart spoil ready for loading.

'So long as the sun is on my shoulders I'm happy,' said Jim. 'But I won't crawl in the earth like a snake, no matter how much I earn for doin' it.'

***

One day there came a rider into the diggings, on a horse still frothing from the gallop. Will had just been to the mine office to collect the weekly cheque from Henry Sutton, and he could tell at a glance that the manager was watching and waiting for someone, glancing constantly out the window.

Will and Henry were both out the front, their business complete, when the rider came, and Will watched as Henry strode out to meet the newcomer, taking a white envelope from the man's hands. He wasted no time in tearing the envelope open and reading the message, then throwing his hat in the air and giving a shout of excitement.

Johnson, by then, had come running from inside the battery shed, so fast and unexpected that Little Blue, who had waited for his owner while the business was transacted, gave a bark and started forward. Will leaned down to restrain him.

'We did it!' called Henry.

Holding Little Blue back with a gentle hand on his chest, Will watched, bemused at what happened next. A wagonette was brought up from a shed and two horses put in the traces. The battery went unattended and the boiler cooled as the workforce set to work carrying Henry Sutton's belongings in trunks and crates from inside his cottage.

Scarcely an hour passed from the arrival of the telegram to when Henry Sutton rode off on his thoroughbred stallion, the wagonette trundling along with two men on the box. By now every digger from the fields had gathered 'round to watch, passing jars of rum, most quite dazed by this turn of events.

A short while later Johnson called all the spectators together. 'Now listen here boys. I'm going to tell you like it is. I'm now the manager here, and the Lyver Hills outfit is, as of a few hours ago, owned by a public company. There ain't much in the way of gold left here, as most of you know. We'll keep the battery going for a week or two, but as soon as the company in London learns the truth I'd reckon that a liquidator will be appointed and the machinery sold off.'

'Where's Henry Sutton gone?' someone called out.

'On his way to Brisbane. By the week's end he'll be on a steamer bound for London. There's no gold left. There'll be no more payments. You might as well all cut your losses and shove off somewhere better.'

Will was glaring at Johnson, the taste of this whole affair bitter in his mouth, despite the fact that only he knew how valuable this property was. The new manager must have noticed this baleful stare, for he walked across and glared down at Little Blue, who was sitting at his master's feet.

'Now that I'm in charge,' said Johnson, 'I won't tolerate animals that can't be controlled. If I see that dog anywhere near my Rossie I'll shoot the bastard.'

Chapter Thirty

Night Journey at Gunpoint

That evening the wind gathered enough strength to chase leaves around the camp, and clouds rallied in, blacking out the stars and moon. Soon afterwards, a steady rain began to fall. The diggers who had dispersed to their camps huddled under tarps, tried to keep cooking fires going, and covered mine shafts as best they could. Heavy rain wasn't good for miners, but they knew how to cope with it just the same.

Water had been in short supply on the Lyver Hills diggings and many of the inhabitants were pleased at first to see the gullies run, filling depressions into pools that would last a while. The problem was that the rain didn't stop. It fell for all of the next day, and then, that second evening, it became torrential. Most of the leases in the lower valley, and the battery site itself were subject to local flooding, and when Will rode over to see if any of the others needed help, water splashed to his gelding's knees.

By midnight the miners were dragging themselves and their belongings to the hilltops, their frightened horses hobbled close-by, while the rain hammered down in drops as heavy as molten lead, and men drank rum, shouted, argued and asked God to 'stop that bloody rain.'

Around midnight, Will, Lainey, Luke, Sam and Jim reluctantly abandoned their lease and joined the others on high ground, leading horses loaded haphazardly with gear and provisions, finding a patch of their own in the long grass and scrub, where they raised a couple of tarps and hobbled their mounts.

Will was wearing the old blue serge Navy jacket he rarely wore in these northern climes, but had once been his trademark. 'I ain't seen rain like this since the Macleay in eighty-four,' said Will, 'and that flooded the whole valley for three weeks.'

'There's no great river here, bloke,' Jim replied. 'Just water on the low ground, an' the gullies runnin'. It'll all go down quick when the rain stops.'

'If the blarsted rain ever stops at all,' said Lainey.

At that moment it didn't seem likely.

It was almost dawn when Will left the shelter of the tarpaulin, his felt hat and old Navy jacket his only protection from the torrent, heading off into the dark of the scrub to relieve himself. He stood in the rain, cursing it, while he unbuttoned his fly and let loose against a tree trunk. He had scarcely fastened back up again when he felt something blunt and hard in the small of his back, that could only be the muzzle of a carbine or handgun.

'Don't move, Will Jones.'

It was Johnson's voice, and there in the miserable rain it carried a terrible menace.

Will froze. He had left the camp unarmed, not intending to be gone for more than a minute. 'What do you want, Johnson? You're playin' a dangerous game pointing guns at people.'

'Dangerous for you, but not me. I know that you and your crew found gold,' Johnson said. 'And now you're gonna take me to where you've been stashin' it.' He paused. 'In case you're thinking of any tricks, I know it's at the Chinaman's garden somewhere.'

'His name's Sam, and you know it,' said Will. 'I'd appreciate if you'd call him that, and anyhow, that garden's bloody miles away. We'd be maniacs to try getting' there in this weather.'

'You an' me are both bushmen. A rainy night never stopped work that needed doing before.'

'I'll have to hunt up my gelding,' breathed Will.

'And let you sick your mates onto me?' laughed Johnson. 'Nah. I've got two saddled horses and a pack down the gully yonder. Start walking, Will Jones, and you can be assured that I'm right behind you.'

From the top of the hill, the slowly lightening sky revealed a landscape of muddy water, with only the piles of spoil and mine headgear still clear. The further side of the valley could not be seen at all, for the rain made it impossible to see more than a quarter mile.

They came to the horses, tethered to trees, the animals sulking at being forced to work in weather like this. Johnson mounted up first, making sure that the barrel of his revolver still covered Will, and fixed the horses together with lead ropes, the pack trailing along behind.

'Now,' said Johnson. 'Lead the way.'

Will glanced back at Johnson, seeing that the revolver remained steady and true in spite of the rain. He had worked with the man on the diggings for some weeks. Johnson was a dogged character, and rarely did he make a threat or promise that he didn't carry through. That revolver was surely loaded, and he would shoot if he had to. With no other option at hand, Will told the horse to walk, and encouraged him with a jab of his heels, heading off in the direction of the garden, three miles of rain and sodden earth away.

He felt the invisible aim of Johnson's revolver as he rode, and prayed that an opportunity would arise to turn the tables.

Chapter Thirty-one

Tracks in the Mud

Little Blue was sitting at the edge of the shelter provided by the tarpaulin, staring out in the direction Will had gone. Now and then he let out a whimper as soft and distressed as a cornered mouse.

'Where the hell has that blarsted Will got to? The dog's havin' a fit,' said Lainey.

'P'raps looking for a horse?' Sam suggested.

But Jim shook his head. He always knew where the horses were. He had a map in his head of their wanderings. He laid the pipe he had been smoking near the fire and rose to his feet. Still with no shirt, his skin spattered with rain, he reached for his Henry rifle, working the lever half-way to check that there was no cartridge in the breech.

'I'll 'ave a scout around,' he said, and left the camp, the dog wasting no time in getting up and walking at his side. Few men could match Jim's ability to see in low light, but this night was gloomier than most, and he had to use every trick to use his eyes to best advantage.

Even so, rain had obliterated most of Will's footprints, and Little Blue proved his worth. He took the scent, padding along with his nose down. Now and then Jim managed to pick out a rain-resistant sign, once even the pale core of a freshly-broken twig.

No more than a hundred yards from the camp, Jim whistled the dog to a stop as they reached one of the many tracks that wound around the hills. In the heavier mud of the trail he clearly saw boot-sized holes, now filled with water. Some belonged to Will, but others appeared to have been made by a man coming from the other direction.

Jim squatted down and placed two fingers into the nearest hole, feeling the depth, aware of Little Blue's presence, whining quietly beside him. He looked around, judging the direction of travel. It seemed to him that the two men had walked together away along the ridge.

'Looks like trouble to me,' said Jim, talking to the dog. 'But we'll find 'im, won't we boy? We gotta follow before the dashed tracks wash away.'

Even in his urgency Jim knew that following on foot and alone would be foolish, so instead he headed back to camp. It took a few minutes of precious time to prime the others, catch horses and tack them up.

Leaving Lainey and Luke to protect their gear, Jim and Sam, with the dog running alongside, rode out of camp and back to where the tracks were slowly disappearing into larger rain puddles. This mattered little to the blue heeler, who found the scent and followed.

Even with the horses at a walk they soon came upon the place where more horses had been waiting, and both Will and the other man had saddled up. There was one boot print near the base of a tree that Jim could see clearly enough to identify as being Will's. Already the two men were throwing up theories and ideas as to what might be happening. It was foul play of some sort. They both knew that. Exactly who and why were still questions that had to be answered.

***

When Johnson and Will Jones reached the high ground above Sam's market garden, dawn was on the way. Just enough light filtered through the clouds to reveal a creek that had already broken its banks, a churning sheet of brown water as wide as a strong man can throw a stone.

The creek flat itself was still above water, but it was dotted with puddles and pools. Will could still see the rows of carrots, tomatoes and leafy vegetables where Sam's caring hands had planted them.

Johnson turned to face Will, the muzzle of his revolver boring into his chest. 'Dismount. You and me are going for a walk down there.'

Both men were saturated, but Johnson's oilskins had kept the rain out better than the serge of Will's navy jacket. Even so, water had run down between necks and collars, through felt hats and into hair and faces. After a hard ride, however, the air did not feel cold, but cloying and warm.

'That's black soil down there,' Will said. 'I don't fancy paintin' me arse in mud, and floppin' around like a lung-fish. You want that gold you're goin' to have to wait until it dries out.'

'You don't unnerstand,' said Johnson. 'I ain't going back. I'm ridin' south, tonight, and taking your gold with me on that packhorse there.' He shook the pistol like a child with a rattle. 'Now get off like I told you, and wait while I fix the horses.'

Will swung down from the saddle. It occurred to him that he might try to run, but he knew enough about Johnson to guess that he was a fine pistol shot who would not hesitate to shoot him down. Besides, it seemed to Will that the game had not run its course. That his best bet was to see this through.

Soon enough, with the horses tethered ready, the two men were walking down the hillside and onto the creek flat, the whispered flow of that waterway mixing with the sound of falling rain.

The mud on that creek flat was even worse than Will had expected. Their feet were soon sinking to the ankles, and each step came with sweat and toil. Sometimes they sloshed through puddles, and when they reached Sam's vegetable garden, the tilled soil was even softer.

'This caper ain't possible,' shouted Will.

Johnson ignored his plea. 'Just find where youse hid it. I know there's a hidey hole somewhere 'ere.'

Will looked at the site. Everything was different. Finding the spot would be challenging, and digging through mud even more so. 'Give it up, you bally idiot.'

'Get down on yer knees, an' start digging,' yelled Johnson.

Will shook his head. He had reached a point where he no longer cared about Johnson and his firearm. Their legs had sunk past their calves and the water was filling the spaces made by their limbs. 'Bugger you. I'm goin' up,' and with that he turned and began the difficult and messy process of walking away. After the third or fourth torturous step he turned back to see that the revolver was again pointing at his back. 'Shoot me mate,' he said, 'but that won't help ya get what ya want.'

Johnson, hesitated, seemed to be about to shoot, then stuck the pistol in the pocket of his oilskin. Now he sank to his knees, tearing at the ground with his hands, scrabbling at it like a dog. 'Damn you Will Jones, I'll find it. I'll find your gold.'

Will ignored him, and continued on, step after step.

He was almost halfway back across the creek flat when he heard a terrible sound. A cataclysmic roar. He looked upstream to see a wall of water churning down along the creek bed. It was a maelstrom, an inland tide of water, carrying trunks of trees and even boulders as it advanced.

At that moment Will was pretty sure that he was about to die. This was not something he could stand against. In that final moment, just before the wall of water hit, he thought of all the things he had not done, and now would never do.

Chapter Thirty-two

The Flooded Creek

Will Jones heard a shout and swivelled his head to see two men on horseback galloping down the hill. Jim was in front, his chest wet with rain, and shining in the gathering light. Sam came behind him, steady and solid, and Will called to them with a whoop.

Yet the swelling rush of water was close now, a flowing moving tide, and Jim reached Will just as it struck, grabbing his arm while the horse dug in, the water washing up over his back, and somehow Will clambered on.

As Jim urged his stallion back towards safety, Will shouted 'Wait,' for he had turned to see Johnson clinging to one of the posts Sam had erected around his vegetable plot, hanging on for dear life, giving out a loud wail of pain as the water dragged at his body. Will could not leave him there to drown, no matter what malice and mischief he had wished on them.

Catching on, Jim urged his mount back towards the stricken man, but Cartridge was losing both his nerve and his depth. Sam's horse was worse, trying desperately to turn and skip back towards dry ground.

'It's too deep,' yelled Jim.

'Just a smidgen closer,' urged Will, and Johnson's eyes were pleading as Will reached out an arm for him.

Johnson hung on by one hand now, extending his other towards Will. Close now. Almost close enough, but the water was still rising and Jim was only keeping control of his mount through near-supernatural horsemanship. Sam for his part, was using his own horse to block the flow, protecting Jim.

Somehow, Will's hand met Johnson's, their fingers touching, then gripping. A momentary expression of relief lit the imperilled man's face.

'Lookout above,' cried Sam.

Will swivelled his head to see that a tree trunk, carried on that flood, was on its way down. For a second it looked as if it would miss them completely, but it spun a little at the last minute, smashing into Johnson, punching into his exposed head and shoulders, tearing him away. His hand was snatched from Will's grip by the force of the current-borne missile.

When the log floated downstream, Johnson went with it.

'Poor barsted,' wailed Will, but their own situation was still precarious. The horses were beyond tired from fighting the mud and water, and Jim leaned down close to his stallion's ear. 'Take us out now boy. Take us up to the hill.'

With Sam's mount matching stride for stride, plunge for plunge, the stallion found his reserves; his will to live. He lunged forward, again and again, over and over until they reached the shadows where Little Blue was swimming beyond his depth but safe, and there was Johnson's dog Rossie as well. There was no fight in them, for the water had become a greater enemy, and all others must take second place.

Jim, Will and Sam rode on up to the stony slope beyond the water and mud, where horses, men and dogs flopped in exhaustion, knowing how close they had been to a terrible death by drowning.

After a time, huddled close for warmth, Will thanked his mates for coming to his side when they did. It was obvious to all of them that he too would be either drowned or close to it by now if they hadn't come along.

And as for Johnson. They did not mention his name, but Will was determined that when the rains stopped, and the flood went down, that he would find the man's body and bury him proper-way. Any man, even one so far off the rails as he, deserved a place to keep his repose in dignity.

Chapter Thirty-three

After the Flood

Even after the rain stopped, and the ground dried, getting the Blue Dog Mine back into production took a few days. The drift and face were filled with thigh-deep water, and removing it all by bucket was an unrelenting labour that even Luke complained about. The soft mud that remained was even more difficult to remove.

Will and his partners were not the only ones having to deal with this issue; most of the shafts in the area were flooded, even those belonging to the big company. There was a sense of unreality across the field, and with Johnson gone, the boiler remained cold and contracts worthless.

When a few groups began to pack up ready to leave, Will decided that he had a responsibility to help hold the place together.

'Them blokes need to know that there's gold down there,' Will muttered into the campfire flames. 'Otherwise they leave this place with pretty much nothin' — ripped off by that damned Sutton an' his kind.'

'You're right,' said Lainey. 'An' we can't let all them investors lose their money. We have to do somefink.'

The next day it was Luke who rode around the camps, calling the diggers together, to assemble on the dry ground beside the stamp mill so 'Will Jones could chew their ears orf about a matter of interest.'

When some fifty or sixty men and a few women had gathered from all around the diggings, some holding shovel handles or bottle necks, some looking friendly and some hostile, Will jumped up on a boulder, and shouted for attention. The crowd hushed up, more or less, and Will held his pipe in one hand like a pointer.

'Orright you fellas,' he said. 'Youse 'ave all heard that old Johnson were drowned like a bandicoot, the other night.' Men nodded and muttered. Some looked towards the battery where the dead man's dog, Rossie, had taken up his old place in the shade, living on handouts from the company men billeted in nearby huts.

Will went on, 'An' youse know that barsted Sutton set us all up, and made a pile by makin' this place look like King Solomon's mines in that stock exchange caper. Well 'e might've just been too clever for his own good.

For the fact is, cobbers, that these hills 'as got a trick up their sleeve. There is gold here, payable gold, on the prodigal leader at least.' Will reached into his pocket and removed a lump of quartz, thickened and heavy with the precious yellow stuff. 'This is from our shaft. There's more where that come from, though we've taken out the best of it.' He tossed the lump to the nearest of the diggers, who caught it with a flick of his wrist, lifted the metal to his mouth and bit down on it.

'By gum,' he shouted. 'That's gold alright.'

There was a cheer and he passed the lump onto the next man.

'Now,' said Will, turning to the ragtag group of men who were employees of the Lyver Hills Company and had been living on rum since Johnson disappeared, unknowing of their employment status. 'You lot get that firebox hot, steam up in the boiler an' bail the shafts ready for work. In a few weeks you can bet that the new company blokes will be here, an' you'll be paid – I'll guarantee that once they see what's under the ground.' He singled out one man, 'Snowy, you're the foreman aren't ya?'

That fair-haired specimen inclined his head. 'Yeah, I'm s'posed to be.'

'Well it's up to you ta get things moving. There'll be ore to process and these men need wages.' Will paused for another cheer, then carried on addressing the main group of diggers, 'Sam reckons that the Prodigal runs rich in a westerly direction from the Blue Dog. Best thing, if you want a slice of it, is to have some of that ground pegged. Jim rode off this morning to fetch the mine warden from Clermont, and he'll be here later to record the claims.'

'What about you, Will Jones?' someone asked. ''Ow do we know you're not just another mongrel tryin' to pick the meat from our tired bloody bones?'

'There's no profit fer me in helpin' you poor cows out. I'm jack of the mining life, and me feet is itchy. When the company people come we'll sell them the claim, and then it's time to ride on. Now go and peg that ground, afore some other barsted does.'

There was a moment's hesitation, then a roar of voices and feet as the diggers headed back to their camps for hammers, string and pegs. Within three hours every possible run of the prodigal leader, excepting the large areas held by the Company, had been pegged, and some had even started digging, in spite of the warden not yet arriving on site.

***

The following day, Will, Luke, and Jim, with Little Blue running alongside, rode down to the creek flat where Sam's garden had been. Half a yard depth of silt had covered the flat over. The garden had disappeared. Logs and drifts of river gravel were scattered here and there.

The three men spread out on horseback, mindful of snakes and noxious, bloated dead stock. The rotten flood smell was thick and cloying.

The task did not take long. Within an hour Will found Johnson's body downstream half a mile. With Jim's help he fashioned a drag-sled from branches and canvas to take him back to dry ground, where they dug a substantial hole in the earth.

They laid him inside and built a neat cairn from surface stones. Luke said a few words over the grave, for he was a churchgoer and remembered a bigger chunk of the Lord's Prayer than the others.

One day, Will decided, he would ride south to the Manning Valley and tell Johnson's people what had become of him and where his remains lay. He was in no rush to do so; it just went onto the list of things he would need to do if the opportunity arose.

***

'So what do we do about our gold?' asked Lainey that night, while the campfire spat sparks, and hissed in the still waterlogged firewood. 'Can't we dig it up an' get paid fer it?'

Will heaved a sigh, and reached a hand down to pat Little Blue, who had come up and sat against his leg. He had been considering the same question himself. 'That would be a fair lump of money to carry around,' he said. 'There's no place in the world that would be safer than under the ground on that creek flat. No one besides us knows that it's buried there, and I'm not ready to give up the road and be a rich man just yet.'

'There's enough gold to buy and stock a proper cattle station, buried under the ground there,' said Luke.

'An' one day that's just what we should do,' said Will, wondering how Lainey's husband had read his dreams so readily. 'But we need to scout around the country more. I ain't quite ready yet.' He looked down at the ground and scraped his boot back and forth across the dust. He knew that there was one thing, more precious than wealth that he needed to find before the time came to settle down.

Chapter Thirty-four

Back on the Trail

Seven weeks after the flood, two board members of the Lyver Hills Mining Company Limited arrived from London via the Port of Maryborough. They rode thoroughbred horses, and were escorted by three hired men. By now these newcomers knew much of what had transpired and expected to find very little at the site – certainly not a bustling rush of busy miners, and increasing optimism, for at least three private shafts had located the prodigal's thick seam already, and the stamp mill was running from the fairy wrens' first chatter to the last cackle of the kookaburras.

Will, having ridden to meet the new arrivals with the foreman of the battery, who had been the unofficial manager for all that time, gave them a quick summary of the situation, including the drowning of Johnson and his own disclosure of the rich seam of gold even Sutton hadn't known about.

'Incredible,' breathed one of the two – a true aristocratic type, with an equine nose and erect posture, whether sitting or standing. 'We had come to believe that the place is worthless—that a fraud perpetrated by two rascally brothers had beggared us all. We came out here to close things down and forestall any further costs.'

'I beg to differ,' said Will. 'The joke's on that barsted Sutton. There's gold here orright, an' I can prove it to youse.'

Will took the English gentlemen down the Blue Dog Mine and showed them the gold-laden vein that ran through it. 'This here leader's named the Prodigal. We reckon it runs on a line from here, an' through all the company leases you haven't yet touched. Sam reckons that there's a ten- or p'raps twenty-year life in the gold within a mile of here. An' this lease right here is for sale.'

'How much?'

'Say one thousand pounds – we've already extracted a tidy parcel of gold, but me partners an' I are tired a' shovel work. We fancy roamin' for a spell an' see where the track takes us. A thousand quid will buy us good nags, provisions, and a stake in whatever we might find along the way.'

The three men shook hands, in that confined space underground, and soon afterwards, back at the camp, the Englishmen sent one of their hired men to the shanty at Wilga for a bottle of grog to seal the deal.

**

By dawn the next morning Will and his crew were already quenching the fire and packing things up, leaving some of the equipment behind.

'Are you sure you won't come with me, back to the farm?' Luke asked Lainey. 'I have to get back. The place will be overrun with weeds and cattle duffers as it is.'

Lainey took his hand. 'Sorry mate, but I can't go back there. The traps would be all over me tryin' to find where Will has got to. Besides, I want to see a little more of the country.'

Luke sat miserably down on a rock, and tears streamed down his face. It was an embarrassing sight, and Little Blue burrowed under his armpit as if to reassure the man that all was not lost. Finally, however, Luke dried his eyes, packed up his things, shook the men by the hand, patted the dog, and kissed Lainey on the cheek. He had his share of the claim sale – two hundred pounds in cash in his pocketbook, and later, one day, there would be a share in the gold buried on the creek flat.

Luke rode south from the Lyver Hills with a downcast look in his eye, knowing for a fact that, like the land they roamed over, Lainey was not to be tamed.

**

A little after noon, Will, Sam, Jim and Lainey set off with eight riding horses and four packs, having seemed to accumulate gear at a great rate since arriving at the diggings. Together they paused at the top of the western ridge, looking down over on the network of leases, shafts and buildings that made up the Lyver Hills diggings.

'One day we'll come back an' dig up that gold we hid,' said Will. 'But 'til then, I don't want to see this place again.'

Sam nodded sagely and Jim was positively glowing at leaving the mine behind.

Finally, with Little Blue padding silently alongside the horses, they headed out into the North West and the frontier country that promised new horizons and wild adventure. New smells and different country, where the traps of New South Wales would never find them; where rules and the men who made them were far away.

Up high, far above them, a circling wedge-tail saw the party set off and watched them for a while, for he knew that riders often startled small game from their crouches and hides. With the sun warm but not too hot, and a cooling breeze from the south, it was a perfect day for riding and flying, and looking for a new life.

More books by Greg Barron, all available at **ozbookstore.com**, good bookshops, and Amazon's Kindle store.

Whistler's Bones
The story of Charlie Gaunt, who rode away from his Bendigo home and joined the famous Durack cattle drive from western Queensland to the Kimberley.

The Time of Thunder
In 1990 two men from across the world, linked by history, converge on Arnhem Land in a bid to solve the fifty-year-old disappearance of a man, and to uncover a Korean War mystery that will have global ramifications.

Camp Leichhardt
Ben Mulligan went down to the Roper River fishing camp to fish for barramundi and find peace. Instead, he found himself caught in a cruel conspiracy, and ultimately fighting for his life.

Outlaw: The Story of Joe Flick
Born in the battleground between two races, Joe Flick is a promising youth. A series of incidents lead him on a path that ends in a bloody tragedy in one of the most beautiful environments on earth.

Red Jack and the Ragged Thirteen
The Ragged Thirteen were a band of thirteen larrikins who put their stamp on Australian folklore with their devil-may-care journey across the wild Northern Australian frontier.

The Last Days of Dom Sebastian
Archaeologists Francis da Costa & Nicolá Massane follow a trail of relics & myth, uncovering a tragic love story, and a voyage past the edge of the known world to Australia's Kimberley.

Galloping Jones and other True Stories from Australia's History
Galloping Jones was a bare-knuckle-fighting larrikin who could tame any horse. Moondyne Joe escaped prison using an ingenious plan that made a whole colony laugh. Based on the popular Stories of Oz history posts, these sketches of Australia's past will inform and entertain you. Above all, they will remind you of what life was like, in the days before highways and smart phones.

All titles are available as eBooks and print copies are always in stock at ozbookstore.com

www.ingramcontent.com/pod-product-compliance
Lightning Source LLC
Chambersburg PA
CBHW010303100726
47904CB00011B/2728